Mr Wilf's Incr

Mr Wilf's Incredible Prank

Pete McGowan

Mr Wilf's Incredible Prank

It was an ordinary day just like any other in the small town of Normantofts and there in a quiet close nestled on the edge of the woods lived Mr Wilf. He was a nice old man who lived alone and he was the sort of fellow that was liked by everyone as he was always jolly and happy to pass the time of day with anyone he met. He always dressed very smart no matter what the occasion, typically in his three-piece tweed suit, matching trilby, a regimental tie and topped off with a fresh carnation in his lapel, yet he was more famously known for his very distinctive handlebar moustache which too was always preened to perfection.

Today was Thursday, but it was no ordinary day for Mr Wilf, Thursday was a very special day to him because it was pension day, or whoopidoo day as he liked to call it and now he had received his pitiful allowance he could at last afford to buy himself his weekly treats. This usually meant a trip down to the shops where he would purchase his weekly ration of best smoking pipe tobacco and especially for his grandchildren who visited nearly every weekend, he would buy a giant bag of mixed sweets, but his most favourite treat of all was his weekly portion of fish and chips and mushy peas.

This particular Thursday Mr Wilf set off to the shops at his usual time with added spring in his step as he was really looking forward to his treat from the sea. However on arriving firstly at Mr Fabooni's off-licence he came across a bunch of unkempt youths that were already congregating there. Mr Wilf immediately recognized them as some of the local boys from the estate who were underage but usually hung around the shops pestering people going in and out to buy them either cigs or alcohol or even both. They were the usual type of boys that every town has, the sort of boys that don't listen to good advice when its given, and rather than staying at home doing something useful with their time, like doing their homework, they would sooner play out late on the streets annoying people by either acting silly or just smashing things.

Mr Wilf being a kindly man, just saw them plain and simply as naughty boys! When Mr Wilf was entering the shop one of these boys in the group shouted to him.

"Hoy Mister, hoy Mister." hearing this Mr Wilf turned around to see what the boy wanted.

"Mister will you buy us some cigs?" "Aww go on mister," some of the other boys pleaded.

Wearing a pleasant smile on his face while tweaking his moustache Mr Wilf replied in a booming but friendly voice so that anyone in the vicinity could hear, "Cigarettes, my goodness you don't want to smoke cigarettes they will stunt your growth and they will make you wheeze like an old man!" The boys didn't like this answer at all, showing their disappointment by making nawrr and tutting noises or mumbling some kind of new swear words but all under their breaths. Noticing but ignoring their displeasure Mr Wilf just laughed it off as though they were an amusement to him and went inside the shop regardless.

On his way out of the shop Mr Wilf was approached by the same group of boys who again pestered him to buy them some cigs.

"Awww go on mister buy us some fags" one pleaded.

Mr Wilf again with a pleasant smile on his face replied, but this time in a quieter and softer voice more like a father talking to a child said,

"Now now boys, smoking is silly, you are just trying to look grown up by smoking but you will end up growing old very fast, don't be in such a hurry" he added, "Life's too short as it is!"

Of course this was just another unsatisfactory answer the boys didn't want to hear let alone try to understand, and one which was also greeted with more disrespectful nawrrs and grunts by the group. By this point they had become so frustrated with Mr Wilf that they started to get cheeky towards him.

"Uh, old like you, how old are you mister, twenty-one" one sarcastically chelped, which brought more jeers and laughter from the other members of the rabble, whose behaviour looked to be getting more unruly by the second.

Mr Wilf just laughed it off and shook his head in disappointment as he proceeded on his way to his next port of call, the fish and chip shop. However on his way out of there and after bidding his usual cheery-bye to the fish shop owner, he was met once again by the same group of persistent boys who by now had decided to become even cheekier towards Mr Wilf.

"Hoy Tashy Face," one shouted. "Can you spare us a quid?" Mr Wilf once again wearing a smile on his face turned to the whole group, but this time he addressed them in a more headmasterly-type of manner and said,

"And what may I ask do you want a quid for?" To which all the group replied in unison, "For some beer."

"Beer" replied Mr Wilf "You are far too young to drink alcohol, it will ruin your lives and you will end up miserable and won't be able to afford nice things, never mind get a job."

On hearing this reply the group of boys grumbled and moaned and finally realizing Mr Wilf wasn't going to play ball and give in to them, they decided to just continue on with their cheek towards him by calling him names as he was walking away, shouting, "IT'S THE WILF, IT'S THE WILF!" "AWOOOOO AWOOOOO!" "IT'S MR TASHY WILF" they blurted. One boy even thought it was funny to screw up some old fish and chip paper from out of the litter bin and launch it sending it flying right past Mr Wilf's ear hole in the hope of making him lose his temper and perhaps give them a chase, which was a bit of a cowardly thing to do really considering Mr Wilf's age. They knew full well that he was hardly up to giving anyone a chase and that he would barely be able to run at all.

As this piece of screwed-up paper flew past his ear hole Mr Wilf suddenly stopped dead in his tracks and swiftly spun around on the spot to confront them, but instead of giving the boys the reaction they wanted, he managed to maintain the same pleasant smile on his face and in a very calm and softly spoken voice, in an attempt to reach their better nature, he said, "Look boys, don't be cheeky to your elders, because remember this and remember it well... you will get old one day!"

He then gave them all a knowing wink and just turned around again and casually walked away towards his home, but this time hopeful of leaving those very thoughts implanted in the boys' minds as he did.

Unfortunately the boys took no heed of his good advice, and in an instant even before it had chance to take root, the boys couldn't resist temptation and almost straight away they reverted back to the name calling as they parted company, but still shouting their defiance non the less! "YOU COULDN'T CATCH US ANYWAY YOU OLD FOGEY, CHEERY-BYE TASHY FACE, HAHAHA" as they returned back to their usual spot outside the shops to annoy someone else.

On hearing that all his wise words were wasted Mr Wilf shook his head in disappointment and continued on his way homeward bound. Even so he couldn't help but laugh and chuckle to himself at all the names the boys had called him, he thought they were quite funny and he just put the whole experience down to a bunch of harmless young boys who had nothing else better to do, and would have to realize their mistakes later on in life.

At that very thought it then suddenly dawned on him that what he had just said to the group of lads, reminded him of an experience he had when he was a young boy.

Through peer pressure and trying to impress older boys he was once showing off and he got a bit too cheeky towards an elderly gentleman and as a result he ended up getting a right slap around the lughole, just before hearing those very same words "You will get old one day!" After that lesson he was never rude or cheeky to his elders again.

It was this memory that stuck in Mr Wilf's mind all of the way home, the lesson he had learned by getting a clout, but how could he make these boys learn that very same lesson he thought. After all he tried speaking to them in every manner he could to make them see sense but that didn't work did it, and he could hardly go around clouting other people's unruly children these days because he would get into trouble with the police! So what could he do he thought!

A Brilliant Idea

On arriving home Mr Wilf quickly polished off his fish and chips and no sooner he had he reached for his best smoking tobacco from the mantelpiece, and after getting comfortable in his old rocking chair he was soon puffing away making smoke rings and pondering what to do.

Hmmmm. "How can I teach those naughty boys a good lesson." He thought and thought, tweaking his moustache at both ends. Then he had a brilliant idea!

You see when Mr Wilf was a young man he used to work building and repairing machines for funfairs and amusement arcades all around the country and after doing this for many years he became a whizz with electronics. So this brilliant idea he came up with was to build a Robot! A Robot that would chase the kids and give them a thrill and a scare at the same time and seeing as he had a ton of leftover spare parts from those days still in his shed, it wouldn't be rocket science to Mr Wilf, it would be easy-peasy he thought, and if he could build a Robot that could chastise the naughty kids in the area, what harm could it do. So with that one conclusion his mind was already made up and off to the shed he went and there he stayed all through the night hammering, sawing, welding and grinding parts. There were flashes and sparks that lit the night sky blue and a few swear words too.

By Friday tea time his creation was finally finished and Mr Wilf was so exhausted he practically slumped into an old leather chair, where after lighting his emergency pipe he kept in the shed, he rested a while to gaze at the marvel he had just created.

The Robot stood about six feet tall when erect with an oblong body just like a slot machine. It had telescopic flexible arms and legs and big circus boots on his feet. It also had a huge pair of leathery wicketkeeper's gloves for hands. Its head had squarish features which tucked away in to its shoulders and although it had oblong eye slits, it had rounded eyes that lit up red. There was also a slot in its chest to put your money in and below it read:

"I'm Chase Me Chase Me, built to thrill and scare your kidz. Put your money in my slot and I will chase them for your quidz!"

Mr Wilf was so excited and pleased with the outcome of his handiwork he couldn't wait to try it out, and the sooner the better he thought.

Appointment with Fear

So a little later on just as it was getting dark, Mr Wilf loaded up his invention into his wheelbarrow and covered it up with an old hessian sack and after he had put on his dark overcoat, he then set off with his invention down to the shops where he intended to place it. All of the short journey he was so very careful to use all the back alleyways to make his way there, so not to be seen.

When Mr Wilf eventually arrived at the shops, he remained in the dark shadows of the alleyway where he firstly peeked around the corner to see if the coast was clear, when he saw that it was, he then very sneakily wheeled his invention to the front of the shop and sited it right next to the bubble-gum machine.

No sooner had he put it there he quickly snuck across the road and keeping his head down low as he did he craftily secreted himself and his wheelbarrow in the bushes to hide, carefully picking a spot where he had the full panoramic view of the shops and his invention, and there Mr Wilf stayed to lay in wait for his intended victims to arrive. While he sat waiting he was so excited he couldn't help chuckling and sniggering away to himself at the very thought of his prank and what might happen, but those chuckles were also accompanied with bit of nervous laughter too, in anticipation that something could go wrong, because he had been in so much of a hurry to carry out his little prank he had skipped all the usual checks and balances and now he was just relying on his usual calculated guessifications, and just hoping everything would go to plan.

Mr Wilf wasn't long in waiting though when he noticed the very same group of naughty boys he'd had a run-in with the night before suddenly appear from around the corner. As the group neared he ducked for cover and he was now having to part the bushes ever so slightly to get a better look, all the while being so very careful not to be seen as he did, after all it would ruin all his hard work!

The boys eventually arrived at the shop and as predicted they congregated in their usual spot right outside the shop entrance and they were soon being their usual selves, annoying customers going in and out of the shops. At first they were all too busy pestering people and acting silly to even notice the new machine, until one of the boys who just happened to be the one who gave Mr Wilf all the lip the night before, eventually spotted it.

"Hoy," he shouted to the rest of the unruly bunch. "Look at this," he said pointing it out to the rest.

Realizing it was the same boy who had called

him Mr Tashy face, Mr Wilf suddenly had to cover his mouth to stop himself bursting into laughter.

The group of boys then quickly surrounded the new machine with one boy already reading out the instructions to the rest, while following the description by the use of the tip of his finger "I'm Chase Me Chase Me built to thrill and scare your kidz. Put your money in my slot and I will chase them for your quidz!"

"Whaaat?!" they all blurted, which was then followed by a sudden burst of laughter.

"Haha haha haha." "Yer funny," one boy shouted.

"Can you believe that?" said another. As far as Mr Wilf could see from the bushes they were all obviously fumbling about in their pockets for a pound coin at the same time and all looking very eager to have a go too, but only the one boy had a pound coin, and again to Mr Wilf's extreme delight it was the same boy who had spotted the machine in the first place, who just so happened to be the same one spoiling for a chase and called Mr Wilf Mr Tashy Face the night before!

This boy then eagerly stepped forward clutching his pound coin to the chorus of "Go on, go on" from his mates who were egging him on from behind.

He then cautiously leant in toward the machine to insert his quid, totally unaware that his every move was being observed by Mr Wilf from across the road, who by this time and still having his hands over his mouth was going purple in the face. Just as the boy was putting the coin in the slot provided, another boy suddenly knocked his hand away before he could, saying, "Wait on a moment, what's this?" pointing out to a little sign at the opposite side of the slot, which they all began to read out loud together.

"Use at own risk, safety definitely not guaranteed."

"Wowwwwww," they all went. "It must be good It sounds like fun to me," said the boy with the quid, who was now more eager to insert his coin. As he did so it was very noticeable from across the street that some of the boys at the back of the group were all getting ready to run just in case. When the boy inserted his pound coin it dropped deep inside the machine, it went "clink clank clunk" as it did! Even Mr Wilf could hear it from across the way.

Within a split second on the very last clunk, his invention burst in to life.

"BADOOPADOO," it went, then it exploded into every colour of flashing light there is, just like a one-arm bandit when it drops the jackpot and accompanied with just about every other noise from an amusement arcade you can hear. Then all of a sudden it raised itself up from the floor exposing its two long legs with a big rubber boot on each one, then its hands and arms popped out from each side and no sooner they had, in a loud Robotic voice the machine began an announcement...

"I'm Chase Me Chase Me, who dares to awake me from my slumber?" Although this was enough to startle anyone, it wasn't quite enough to faze this group just yet, until its head popped out of its shoulders on a long telescopic neck, then suddenly thrusting it's robot mush right up to the boy's face, it said "Was it you? I've got your number!" which really did startle the boy and made him jump back a couple of feet. Then all of a sudden and to all the boys' amusement Chase Me Chase Me began running on the spot, and it looked as though it was warming up just like an athlete would do. At first it looked quite harmless, so much so it made all the boys laugh, that is until the Robot began to announce its final warning...

"Are you ready, you better be because here I come in five seconds... five... four...

By this time the boys were already legging it down the road, but as they did and because they hadn't anticipated that they were going to be chased by a slot machine, a couple of the boys must have been a bit more scared than the others and they couldn't help trumping as they ran, which was so funny to the rest of the group none of them could hardly run for laughing. They only managed to get about thirty yards away from the shop when they had to pull up and stop, but on looking back to see what they were actually running from, they were just in time to see Chase Me Chase Me deliver its final warning, announcing:

"HERE I COME!," as it leaped from its position faster than a greyhound leaving its trap and with its knees nearly touching its Robot chin it came bounding up the road towards them, CLOMP, CLOMP, CLOMP it went, with its arms flailing wildly in the air and its eyes now glowing red and if that wasn't scary enough, there was also an added sound effect that Mr Wilf had taken from an old ghost train ride, which went "WHOOO-HOOO-HAHAHA".

On seeing this terrifying sight of a demented Robot heading towards them clomping up the street with its big boots, the boys were off like the clappers with their feet barely touching the ground and all of them were trumping this time, but none of them were laughing now! They were making baa lamb noises instead and bleating

"Maaaam, maaaamy!" as they fled.

Mr Wilf was so excited at seeing the spectacle he had created that he completely forgot himself for the moment, when he suddenly stood up from out of the bushes and began mimicking the robots actions by running on the spot and flailing his arms in the air, just like he had programmed it to do and began laughing uncontrollably. He was so pleased with his prank and he thought it couldn't have been going any better.

That is until Chase Me Chase Me caught up with the back stragglers of the group who looked like they had run out of wind – probably due to their silly smoking habits or maybe they were just too restricted by the silly low-cut pants they all wore hanging below their bottoms – who were now making louder baa lamb noises the nearer Chase Me Chase Me got to them. And as the robot did, one by one they each got their ear holes walloped by its big leathery hand – "WALLOP, WALLOP, WALLOP" it went as each got a clout.

One boy got such a wallop he was sent spinning like a top and fell into someone's household waste bin and scattered all of its contents everywhere. Another was walloped so hard he was sent flying head first straight into Normantofts' notoriously named Black Beck, which was always known to be full of big black slugs. The other boys were lucky enough to escape with just a sore ear hole each, which sent them running home to tell their mums and dads.

When it caught up with its intended victim, the boy who had inserted the coin, Chase Me Chase Me swiftly snatched him up by the scruff of the neck so quick the boys legs were still running mid-air, to which he began to shout his protest

"GEROFF, GEROFF, PUT ME DOWN" which just happened to be one of the safety commands Mr Wilf had installed in Chase Me Chase Me's memory in case someone got too scared. On hearing this safety word, Chase Me Chase Me automatically came to an abrupt halt, and still holding the boy aloft, its Robot voice then said, "Your wish is my command." However, instead of putting the boy down on the ground like it was supposed to, it instead dropped him and in mid-air punted him with his big rubber boot up the backside, which went "flump" as it did, launching him through the air and right across the other side of the road, where he went flying over a garden fence and straight in to a washing-line full of ladies underwear, landing head first in a pair of Mrs Spingle's best bloomers.

On seeing his Robot do this Mr Wilf wasn't jumping up and down on the spot any more, he was now stood with his hands holding his head speechless and could only watch as Chase Me Chase Me then did an about-turn and to the theme tune of Rocky blurting from out of its inbuilt speakers, it began jubilantly skipping back towards the shop while gesturing with its big thumbs to the lit-up sign on its back which read, "What's my name?" as it returned to its spot right next to the bubble-gum machine.

"That wasn't supposed to happen, that wasn't

supposed to happen," repeated Mr Wilf frantically as he dashed across the road to retrieve his invention as fast as he could, all the while hoping that he hadn't been seen, he then hurriedly loaded up his invention back in the wheelbarrow and covered it with the old sack again, then snuck stealthily back in to the dark alleys from which he came, and rushed towards home as fast as he could.

The whole incident didn't last more than a couple of minutes, but it managed to cause quite an uproar in the street. There was a right commotion, neighbours were out shouting about all the noise, and parents were out shouting at their naughty boys who were still crying, dogs were barking and there was litter strewn everywhere.

In only a short moment of time there was a small crowd of people gathered in the street and while everyone was trying to make sense of what had just happened, Mrs Spingle was out in her garden prodding what she thought was an intruder with a brush pole, who was now suspended upside-down with his head protruding from a leg-hole of her best Sunday drawers. She was shouting, "GET OUT, GET OUT OF THERE GET OUT YA PERVERT!." and at every prod she gave, the boy was screaming, "Ouch, ouch stop it."

It was now getting a little bit more heated in

the street too, neighbours began to fall out with neighbours, who started falling out with the parents, who were falling out with the other parents, who were also shouting at their boys, "ROBOT, ROBOT! TELL ME ANOTHER ONE LIKE THAT AND I WILL GIVE YOU ANOTHER THICK EAR!"

The more the boys tried to tell their incredible story the angrier their parents got and all to moans from their surrounding neighbours.

"It's always your boys... nothing but trouble," one said.

"Always trouble this lot," said another.

"Don't blame my lad," one parent snapped and before you knew it they were all arguing with each other about who was to blame. Fortunately before things could get anymore heated, it was all soon cooled down by the sudden appearance of a certain Sergeant Grimper, who just happened to be passing by on his bike on his way to the station to start his nightshift.

"Now then, now then, what's all this" he said marching into the thick of the matter and taking control of the situation as policemen do. Only after a short while of listening to what the boys had to offer up as an explanation and bearing in mind each of them was now indeed sporting a big glowing red ear hole apiece, quickly resulted in Sgt Grimper frog marching who he thought were the two main ringleaders, followed by their mums and dads down to the shops where the boys had convinced them all that there was indeed a Robot. The trouble was on arrival at the shop, there was no Robot, it wasn't there was it? There was nothing else but a bubble-gum machine.

"Right that's it," one of the boys' parents snapped. "You're grounded for a month you little liar," which was immediately echoed by the other boys' parents who were probably trying to look more responsible by responding with a two months grounding instead. As a result of this and not wanting to be outdone or look less lenient in front of Sgt Grimper, the other boy's parents increased their bid to "Three months". However, before their bidding could escalate and turn into some kind of punishment auction, it was conveniently brought to an abrupt end when interrupted by the sudden sound of Mr Fabooni's shop doorbell as he came outside to close the shutters for the night.

"Mr Fabooni, Mr Fabooni," one of the boys blurted in desperation, which got his attention straight away and everyone else's too!

"What's the matter kid?" asked Mr Fabooni. "Tell my mum and dad about that machine that turns into a Robot and chases kids for a quid that was outside your shop, go on tell them Mr Fabooni" he said more than sure that he would back up their story and clear the whole matter up.

Only to hear him say, "Whaaat? What are you on

about now? A machine that turns in to a Robot?" Mr Fabooni's face was a picture of puzzlement as the boy desperately repeated, "That Robot that chases kids for a quid Mr Fabooni," hopeful that he at least knew something about it, but all the while fearing a lengthy grounding coming his way.

"Look kid, I've got a bubble-gum machine that's all," said Mr Fabooni.

"There I told you he was a little liar," the boy's father snapped, only to hear Mr Fabooni go on to make things worse

"Your kids are crazy, they're going to send me to the nuthouse one day, these boys are always trouble hanging around my shop," adding, "I think they have only made this up because I won't sell them booze and cigarettes."

On the parents hearing those fateful words a deadly silence fell, you could hear a pin drop, followed by a cold gust of wind.

Then came the reaction and it was loud "BOOZE!... CIGARETTES!..." each parent screamed in disbelief, followed by, "Right that's it," as they went to grab their boys by the scruff and drag them off home. It was at this point everyone was loudly interrupted by Sgt Grimper who had stayed quiet for the time being while he weighed the situation up, but now he came stepping in.

"No that isn't it, I think I will have a say in this matter now... and I think I have a say in the punishment too," said the Seargent. On hearing this intervention it was the parents turn to be silent and they were all now expecting the worst, the boys gulped and their mums and dads did too as Sgt Grimper went on to say, "Now then, I expect to see each and every last one of you, I've got your names here in my book," he said, "in church this Sunday and every Sunday for the next three months."

Believe it or not there wasn't one grumble, not a sound from any of them, they just accepted what they thought fair and light punishment from Sgt Grimper, who also went on to say, "Now get yourselves home before I change my mind" – which they all quietly and humbly did without question or argument. But before they could get out of earshot of Sgt Grimper, it wasn't without hearing him add at the quick request of Mr Fabooni, "And you and your mates are all banned from the shops too."

Meanwhile, after fleeing the scene in such a hurry Mr Wilf reached home in no time at all. He came crashing through the back garden gate, using his wheelbarrow to open it, straight across the lawn and into his shed, closing the door behind him. Once inside he let out a huge sigh of relief and practically fell into the old armchair with exhaustion. His heart was racing in his chest and beads of sweat were now running down his nose so fast his moustache drooped and was beginning to look more like the character Fu Manchu than Fu Manchu did and because he hadn't stayed around to see the outcome of his prank he was now starting to feel like that villain too, so he began wringing his hands together repeatedly saying, "Oh dear, oh dear, what have I done, I'm in trouble now, I'm in trouble now" and he definitely wasn't his usual jolly self.

This was because Mr Wilf had never been in trouble with the police before and he didn't know how he would handle it if he ever was, so in fear of that, he then started to point the finger of blame at his invention instead, saying, "No, no, it's you that's in trouble, you Chase Me Chase Me, you're a very naughty Robot, you weren't supposed to do that, you've let me down," he said, wagging his finger at the same time. Yet all the while Mr Wilf knew in his heart he was just talking to bits of steel and plastic and a few bits of wire that he had thrown together in his shed and it was his responsibility to take any blame, if any was to come.

After only a short while when Mr Wilf had calmed down a bit and come to his senses, he then took Chase Me Chase Me from out of the wheelbarrow and plonked it down in the corner and covered it with the old sack for the night and just before he closed the door behind him he turned towards Chase Me Chase Me and said, "You're a very naughty Robot, but after a few more adjustments tomorrow you'll be as right as rain." He then gave Chase Me Chase Me a reassuring wink, said good night and turned off the shed light and headed back inside the house. Once indoors he wasted no time in making his usual hot mug of milk, he then loaded up his pipe and sat in his favorite rocker to relax and reflect on everything that had happened.

After thinking about the whole incident it wasn't long before Mr Wilf was back to his normal jolly self and laughing again, further amusing himself by mimicking the same baa lamb noises the boys were making while running up the road from his invention. It wasn't too long either before Mr Wilf couldn't help making some other farm animal noises himself, while snoring his head off fast asleep in bed.

The very next day Mr Wilf was up bright and early and having slept very well he was in a jolly mood singing and making his breakfast. Halfway through eating his boiled egg and soldiers though, the events of the night before came flooding back in his mind, which instantly reminded him that he not only had to do some extra work on his invention, but he also thought he had better check something more important out first. After eating breakfast he jumped out of his chair, put on his hat and coat and headed straight down to the shops as quick as he could.

On arrival and entering the newsagents the doorbell rang as usual, but he wasn't ready for the unexpectedly rapturous welcome he received from Mr Fabooni, when he practically pounced on him from behind the greeting card stand.

"Good morning, good morning Mr Wilf how are you today, ha haa haha? I've never seen you this early before Mr Wilf, what can I do for you sir," he said in his usual Italian accent, which wasn't real, but which he always kept out of tradition from the days his mum and dad ran the ice cream parlor there – he was actually born here in Yorkshire!

"Err, err," Mr Wilf stuttered, struggling to think of an excuse to be there after being put on the spot by Mr Fabooni, so he quickly replied with the first thing that came into his head. "Have you got a morning paper?"

Mr Fabooni, now having a curious look on his face then replied, "Yes I've got lots of morning papers, which one would you like?"

"Err, err, that one," said Mr Wilf, pointing to the first one he saw on the rack.

Of course Mr Wilf didn't really want a morning paper at all, his early visit was just a ruse to find out if his little escapade the night before had been rumbled.

"The Horsey Times?" Mr Fabooni exclaimed in disbelief. "I didn't know you were into gambling and that sort of thing."

"Oh just give me a morning paper," snapped Mr Wilf irritably, but purposely acting as though he got muddled and it was a natural mistake to make and he wasn't there for any other reason than to buy a newspaper?

On noticing his confusion Mr Fabooni was getting even more puzzled by the second, which prompted him to say, "It's funny, I've never known you buy a morning paper here before." but then with a smile on his face he jokingly added,

"You haven't been up to no good and got yourself in the papers have you haha haha?"

This made Mr Wilf laugh, but not quite as much as Mr Fabooni, who thought it was hilarious.

"Hahaha... No, no just trying to keep up with the world's events," replied Mr Wilf, trying normalize the conversation, but also enquiring, "Why, what have you heard?" To which they both automatically burst into the loudest of laughter.

"Awww, you crack me up Mr Wilf," said Mr Fabooni, thinking he was just joking. "Hahaha. Nothing Mr Wilf... nothing ever happens around here hahaha, just the same old, same old, hahaha," laughed Mr Fabooni.

Mr Wilf was so very relieved to hear this, he became much more relaxed now that nothing had been mentioned about the night before, so he was quite happy to pay for his paper and bid his usual farewell of cheery-bye to Mr Fabooni, and be on his way.

However, just as Mr Wilf had opened the door ready to leave, Mr Fabooni shouted at the top of his voice to anticipate the noise of the traffic outside, "EXCEPT ABOUT THAT ROBOT THAT WENT AROUND ATTACKING PEOPLE LAST NIGHT, AND THEY HAD TO CALL THE ARMY OUT TO TRY AND CATCH IT!"

On hearing this news, Mr Wilf stopped dead in his tracks, and thinking the game was up he slowly closed the door in front of him. Now resigned to his fate he turned to face Mr Fabooni and almost trembling with worry he was just about to confess his involvement in case something serious had happened, when he was hugely relieved to see a massive grin on Mr Fabooni's face instead.

"Aww it was crazy," Mr Fabooni went on to say. "It was only those crazy kids who hang around my doorway, they had made up a story about a Robot that was outside my shop and it chased them, and they told the police all about it".

"The police?" interrupted Mr Wilf. Yes, Sgt Grimper."

"Sgt Grimper?" Mr Wilf again interrupted.

"Yes, they told him the Robot was mine and they tried to put some kind of blame on me."

"So no one believed them?" replied Mr Wilf

"Of course not" said Mr Fabooni. "Derrrr."

"Are you ok Mr Wilf?" enquired Mr Fabooni sensing that something wasn't quite right,

"Yes... yes I'm fine, thank you very very much

indeed," replied Mr Wilf, who was so relieved to hear the great news that he was definitely in the clear, he wasted no time in again bidding his usual cheery-bye farewell as he hastily left the shop.

Once again Mr Wilf was back to his normal jolly self and he practically skipped all the rest of the way back home without a care in the world as he did.

Decision Time

On arrival home Mr Wilf had lots to think about, after he had finished his cup of tea and cheese and onion crisp sandwich he lit his pipe and sat in his favourite rocking chair to ponder what to do next.

"What to do... what to do?" he said to himself. "Do I fix or dismantle Chase Me Chase Me?" He thought long and hard, because although it was his creation it could have got him in to lots of bother and now that he had no need to scare anyone's kids anymore, was it worth the trouble to keep it? There he sat tweaking the ends of his handlebar moustache with a bit of old-fashioned spit thinking.

It wasn't long before Mr Wilf's mind was made up, he jumped from out of his rocker, grabbed his keys off the window sill, and went straight outside towards his shed, but when he got there the shed door was already open?

"Hmmm I remember locking that last night," he said to himself, and curious to find out why this was, he cautiously peered inside. At first sight everything looked to be as it should, Chase Me Chase Me was still in the place he had put him, and nothing else seemed out of order, but why was the door open he thought. On closer inspection Mr Wilf noticed that the door lock mechanism was unscrewed and it had been removed from the inside, not only that his screwdriver was also missing from out of its usual stand. Then looking over towards Chase Me Chase Me he noticed something else, the Robots lead was plugged in the wall socket and it was also on charge!

"Hmm that's strange, I don't remember doing that" he muttered, but things were about to get even stranger, when he happened to glance over at his invention, he thought he could see one of its eyes watching him through a hole in the old hessian sack that he had covered him with the night before. Noticing this Mr Wilf leant forward for a closer look to make sure his eyes weren't playing tricks on him, he slowly reached out and as quick as a flash he snatched away the sack, but in that instance he did he was almost sure he saw Chase Me Chase Me's head drop back down into its shoulders. Which automatically made Mr Wilf think that it was as though Chase Me Chase Me had been watching him all of the time, with this thought in mind it made the hairs prickle down the back of his neck. In spite of that Mr Wilf was a logical man and he knew the machine was just an invention he had knocked up from the old left over spare parts that were in his shed, so he quickly dismissed any of those notions out of his head, and put it down to his old age and his eyes playing tricks on him.

Nonetheless, still bearing in mind what he thought he had seen, he quickly unplugged its battery charger... just in case!

Mr Wilf then picked up a screwdriver and began to investigate by opening the Robot's chest panel where he began to poke around with the screwdriver and make an inspection. The first thing he noticed was that the coin box was empty, but then he saw the reason why, the pound coin the boy had put in the night before was jammed solid higher up in the mechanism and to his surprise, it was a dodgy pound coin too!

"The little rotter, so that's why it jammed," he muttered, but it didn't explain the reason for Chase Me Chase Me's unexpected malfunction and strange behavior, he thought. So Mr Wilf then proceeded to investigate further, by putting his head right inside Chase Me Chase Me's chest cavity for a better look around and a tinker.

However with every tinker Mr Wilf made with his screwdriver, his invention flinched.

"There... there" said Mr Wilf reassuringly each time it moved, not only to calm the Robot but himself too! It had just occurred to him at that very moment with his head deep in the Robot's chest cavity, that because the pound coin was jammed where it was and the fact his invention was fully charged, it could only mean one thing… Chase Me Chase Me was fully operational and could burst in to life at any moment.

Mr Wilf now began to proceed very cautiously.

"Hmmm," he thought, looking at the jammed coin, wondering whether he dare to give one last jab with his screwdriver, but rather than risk activating its mechanisms and becoming Chase Me Chase Me's next victim, he decided to just remove its memory board instead, and that would be that he thought. So he slowly reached for its memory card to pull it out, but it was tight in its slot and when he tried to yank it free, Chase Me Chase Me flinched and its arm popped out from one side and its hand then suddenly pinched Mr Wilf's bum! It gave him so much of a fright it made him jump up and bang the back of his head inside the Robot's chest, causing him to drop his screwdriver which fell deep inside of Chase Me Chase Me's workings and straight into its main control unit, causing all its circuits to short out.

There was a big blue flash of light and a loud bang, followed by a really loud shriek from Mr Wilf as he came flying out backwards through the air and landing in a big heap on the shed floor. His face was black and his grey-white hair was now standing on end, with wisps of smoke even coming out of his ears.

Mr Wilf just sat there in so much of a daze he could do nothing but only watch as Chase Me Chase Me then began to shake and judder out of control, by the time Mr Wilf came around enough to pick himself up off the floor, his invention suddenly burst into life.

"BADOOPADOO!" it went, with all of its lights flashing and making every amusement arcade noise you can think of as it went straight into the programmed routine it was supposed to do, but for some reason it had already began jumping up and down on the spot and now too late for Mr Wilf to even try to stop it.

"I'm Chase Me Chase Me, who dares wake me from my slumber?" it then announced.

On hearing this Mr Wilf was now in full panic mode because he knew what was coming next and seeing as he had no way now of locking the shed door he was now prepared to do almost anything at this point to prevent his invention from getting out. So in desperation he pushed the old leather club chair and a pair of step ladders in front of the door way to try to block its way, only then to hear the Robot which was now standing in front of him, say "Was it you Tashy Face? I've got your number," at the same time pushing its Robot's mush right into Mr Wilf's face as it did.

Although Mr Wilf was expecting it to do exactly this, he was more than surprised to hear the audacity of what his invention had just said, to which he instantly rebuked in return "WHAT DID YOU JUST SAY?" in that very instant the Robot jumped back a couple paces and then it started to come out with all sorts of nonsense, as though it had gone mad. Its arms began waving about in the air and then it started running on the spot, saying daft things like, "Giz a cig mister," "Hoy lend us a quid," and "Give us a chip darling" then it's lights lit up and began to flash all over with bells ringing like someone had dropped the jackpot again... then all of a sudden its lights went completely out, it fell totally silent and stopped dead still. On seeing this and assuming it had conked out, Mr Wilf was confident enough to dare approach it again to try and remove its memory card and permanently disable it, but as he put his hand inside to grab it, the Robot suddenly fired up again, but this time to deliver its final warning,

"You better get ready to run, because here I come in five seconds... five... four..."

On hearing this terrifying count down it left Mr Wilf no other choice but to take drastic measures, and as a last resort he quickly made a grab for the nearest heavy object to hand with the intention of clobbering the robot and putting it out of action, which just happened to be an old fire extinguisher he had taken from an RAF airplane and on noticing what it was and hoping it still worked, instead of clobbering his invention, he pointed it at the Robot just as it said the final words of "Here I come," and it made its first move, Mr Wilf managed to release the safety pin in the nick of time and pull the trigger. In that instant there was a loud "Whooooooosh" sound as the foam gushed from out of its nozzle, splattering Chase Me Chase Me and completely covering it from head to foot with pink foam, which expanded so much on contact it came flooding out of the shed door and with it came Mr Wilf too! He was now covered head to foot in thick sticky pink fire-retardant foam that was used in the war to put out flames when bombers crashed on landings and take-off.

Mr Wilf quickly got straight to his feet and immediately began to wipe the foam from his eyes, just in time to see Chase Me Chase Me come flying out of the shed like a big pink marshmallow with its arms still flaying in the air and because it couldn't see where it was going it was now bumping into everything in the garden and each time it did it shouted, "You naughty boy, you naughty boy" until it finally crashed into Mr Wilf's hundred-gallon water butt, knocking it clean from its stand, which burst wide open on impact, sending a massive tidal wave of water across the garden lawn picking up both Mr Wilf and Chase Me Chase Me who was now sitting on Mr Wilf's chest riding the crest of a wave in a deluge of water, flushing them straight into the greenhouse and right into Mr Wilf's prize tomato plants. Although the water helped to swoosh the pair free of sticky foam, they were both now covered in compost, netting and plants instead.

Mr Wilf wasted no time in trying to get out of his tangle as quick as he could, unfortunately Chase Me Chase Me had beaten him to it, and in an instant it had already jumped to its feet, and its Robot voice then said "Cheery-bye Mr Wilf, catch ya later" and then it just set off bounding down the garden path and jumped over the six foot garden fence with the skill of an athlete... with ease.

By the time Mr Wilf got out of his tangle and to his feet again his Robot had already run straight across the corn field, through a barbed-wire fence and gone crashing through the trees and straight into Spooker's Wood. There were pheasants honking and birds and feathers and leaves flying everywhere.

Leaving Mr Wilf nothing else to do but watch in disbelief as his invention finally disappeared into the undergrowth.

"Well, well, well, I wasn't expecting that," he said while scratching his head, and for a while he just stood there staring at the path his Robot had carved through the field and trees, trying to figure out what just happened, but also to listen for any sign of his Robot's return just in case.

After about half an hour had passed, Mr Wilf came to a logical conclusion that because Chase Me Chase Me had only two hours' worth of battery lifespan on board, plus the fact that it was now dragging about twenty metres of barbed-wire fence, it would soon wear down it's charge, or at the very least it would tangled up in the gauze somewhere and get stuck. He also concluded that it was more than likely it would fall down one of the old abandoned mineshafts that were in the woods and because it was private property and the barbed wire fence Chase Me Chase Me was dragging was there to keep people out, it was very unlikely to come across anyone else in there. So he was more than sure now his invention wasn't coming back and that would be the last he would see of it.

Out of Sight out of Mind

Reassured by those thoughts Mr Wilf decided to pay it no more mind and with that conclusion he went back in to his house. His mind now turned to other things like making his dinner and even more importantly preparing the snacks for tomorrow's garden party he had planned for his grandchildren's weekly visit.

Mr Wilf was a thoughtful man who enjoyed every moment of being with his family, he always made the extra effort to make their day fun and everyone had a good old time. So on his itinerary (list to do) he had to make buns and a trifle and prepare lots of snacks and nibbles and of course everyone's favourite, his homemade fruit punch cordial. Afterwards he planned to put George's football practice nets out on the lawn and pick up the bouncy castle from the Dog and Ferret, which Bill the landlord was lending him.

No sooner had Mr Wilf finished his dinner he set about getting all of these jobs done and when they were he wasted no time in setting off with his wheelbarrow down to the pub. Where on arrival there he firstly loaded up the bouncy castle from the beer garden before going inside, as he thought it was fair to buy Bill the landlord a pint for the free lend of the bouncy castle, and of course a little taste for himself, well it was the least he could do!

"Ho, hello there Mr Wilf are you all set then?" Bill the landlord asked.

"Ho yes, thank you very much Bill, can I buy you a pint?" Mr Wilf enquired.

"Don't mind if you do," replied Bill knowingly, with a pint glass already waiting in his hand. So after a few more pleasantries Mr Wilf went to his usual place in a quiet corner of the pub to relax, because it was rather busy at the bar on account of it being the weekend and he just wanted to sit by himself. After all he'd had a very stressful day!

As he was sitting there though, quaffing on his pint and trying to keep the foam off his moustache and just as he was getting comfortable, the pub door suddenly came crashing open and startling everyone in the process, when this little old man came spilling inside and nearly falling to the floor.

"Help, help," he cried, making the once noisy pub suddenly fall silent. It was old Mr Snooby the retired postman.

"There... there... in Spooker's Wood," an out of breath Mr Snooby spluttered, whilst leaning against the bar trying to gain his composure, but still managing to gesticulate with his finger that was pointing outside.

"Now now slow down, take your time," said Bill, handing him a glass of medicinal brandy.

"Get that down ya, and tell us what on earth the matter is Mr Snooby?" Which he did and in one gulp too, before trying to gather his words with practically everyone else in the room now encouraging him on.

"Go on, go on Mr Snooby tell us more," they all urged, so Mr Snooby went on to tell them.

"Well," he said, "I was out in Spooker's Wood trying to shoot something for mi supper (which really meant illegally poaching for game birds) and I was knelt down and lining my sites up on this pheasant, when all of a sudden something, something...." Mr Snooby paused for a moment, still trying to regain his composure,

"Go on Mr Snooby," a couple of impatient listeners demanded, only to hear him say, "Something came up behind me and kicked me up the arse and I went flying through the air and landed in a big deep hole!"

"Something?" everyone questioned "What do you mean something?" "Down a hole?" another said, while the rest were just urging him to go on with the tale, which he did but not until Bill the landlord encouraged him with another medicinal brandy he had in the waiting. After another gulp of that he continued. "Well, I managed to climb out of this deep hole, but when I did, just as I got to the top there stood over me was this..."

Mr Snooby paused again and took a big gulp of

his liquid courage and then he just blurted it out: "A Robot!"

"A Robot, a Robot," everyone echoed in disbelief, followed by a huge cry of laughter. Which again wasn't too surprising considering the tale he told. But one man in the room wasn't laughing at all, and that was Mr Wilf who was instead sat with his head in his hands peering through his fingers and muttering repeatedly, "Oh dear... I'm for it now, I'm for it now".

Fortunately to Mr Wilf's relief, Bill the landlord decisively intervened when he said, "Now, now, come on Mr Snooby, it's not another one of your tales is it, remember the last one you told us about a spaceship that landed there not so long ago..."

"No... no... it's true," snapped Mr Snooby in his defense, desperately trying to further explain, but all the while he was trying to elaborate on his tale, he kept getting interrupted by the other merry customers making sarcastic comments like:

"Why didn't you shoot it for your supper then?" which was very funny and got quite a few laughs all round, but not half as funny as Mr Snooby's answer to that very question, which was, "I couldn't shoot it because it took my gun and bent it around a tree and then threw it down that deep hole!"

Well, at this incredible reply the whole room

erupted into the loudest belly laughter anyone could ever make, it was so loud it practically drowned out poor old Mr Snooby's pleas for them to listen. The more he pleaded the louder the laughter got and the ribbing jokes came thick and fast, as this once sympathetic group of listeners had now turned into a mocking crowd.

This was all good news to Mr Wilf though, he was more than pleased hearing everyone's reaction to poor old Mr Snooby's story.

Taking advantage of the situation Mr Wilf got up and quietly slipped out of the side door unnoticed, collected his loaded wheelbarrow from the back of the pub and headed straight for home. All the way back he couldn't help laughing and chuckling to himself, thinking about poor Mr Snooby's experience in the wood and the response he got telling the other customers in the pub.

The icing on the cake for Mr Wilf was that no one took Mr Snooby seriously at all. Reassured by that and also calculating that Chase Me Chase Me's batteries would definitely be flat by now, especially after its latest performance with Mr Snooby, he was sure now it would be the last he would hear of it.

On arrival home Mr Wilf parked up the loaded wheelbarrow and seeing as he'd had quite a busy and eventful day, he decided to skip his usual smoke on his pipe and just have his hot mug of milk which always made him sleep soundly and soon afterwards he was in bed and snoring until morning.

The Garden Party

The next day came fast as it usually does when you've had a nice sleep, and it was a really nice and sunny morning too, just perfect for Mr Wilf's garden party. He was so excited he was up and about bright and early and he wasted no time at all in setting everything up for his planned day and smiling all the while he was doing it. Yesterday's events never even entered his mind at all, he was too busy preparing the fun day ahead.

No sooner had Mr Wilf completed his very last job, which was to blow up the bouncy castle, the doorbell rang and within seconds all Mr Wilf's family came rushing in to receive hugs from their Granddad, all very happy to see him as usual and looking forward to their fun day.

They really appreciated how much their Granddad loved to see them and the lengths he went to make their visit fun, especially the grandchildren who were highly delighted to see the bouncy castle, to shouts of "Excellent" and "Proper good" from them all.

There was George and Charlie, their mum and dad, Evie and her mummy, and little Molly the youngest and her mum and dad. All the kids wasted no time at all removing their shoes and were soon bouncing away on the castle while the mums and dads were tucking in to lovely grub and lashings of Granddad Wilf's homemade summer fruit punch cordial.

Everything was just perfect and everyone was thoroughly enjoying themselves. Later on in the day while the adults were still relaxing or having a nap, the kids were still pretty active in the garden and although Granddad Wilf had been keeping a watchful eye on them, he couldn't help himself nipping into the kitchen to get some more trifle. However on his return he noticed that someone was missing? George was practicing his football skills on his five-a-side nets, and Evie was showing little Molly how to make daisy chains in the garden, but there was no sign of Charlie.

"Hmmm, where is that little rascal" he muttered to himself, because Charlie was what he called a 'little rooter', constantly rooting in Granddad's stuff and finding things that weren't lost and searching in places where his Granddad did actually keep dangerous things too! Bearing this in mind he had a quick look around, at first sight he noticed that the shed door was open.

"Ha haaa," said Grandad and in that instant he struck a Ninja pose and he began to creep towards the shed on his tiptoes. This didn't go unnoticed by the rest of his family, who were now watching Granddad with bemused looks on their faces, as he was now tweaking his moustache and grinning like a Cheshire cat.

Then without warning he suddenly pounced into the shed shouting, "GOT YA!" But only to come back out empty handed, Charlie wasn't in there. So now Granddad and soon everyone else was shouting,

"Charlie where are you?" as one would do when someone is hiding and they were searching all the possible places where he might be. Suddenly everyone heard Charlie's little voice shouting, "Granddad, I'm up here," and when everyone turned in the direction to see where it was coming from, they saw to their utter astonishment that little Charlie was right at the top of Granddad Wilf's prize apple tree, and now that he had been seen he began shouting even louder, "GET ME DOWN, GET ME DOWN."

So everyone quickly hurried down the garden to his rescue, his mum shouting hysterically,

"Don't you move, we'll get you down!" Once at the foot of the tree Charlie's Dad immediately put his brother George onto his shoulders to stand up and reach the branch where Charlie was sat. The trouble was that when George got up there himself, Charlie started to feel safe in George's company and now he had suddenly decided he didn't want to come down anymore.

To make matters worse, well for Granddad that is, Charlie and George had also decided to start munching on his prize apples too and the funny thing was they both could hardly munch for laughing at the sight of their Granddad Wilf's concerned face watching them.

"Right that's it, I know what to do," said Granddad, as he desperately headed back up to the house to get the ladders, while muttering something about his prize apples under his breath – when all of a sudden a couple of apple cores flew overhead.

"You're for it now, you pair of monkeys,"... "You're for it now," Granddad jokingly laughed, none the less it made him make more haste to get the ladders before all his apples were eaten.

No sooner had Mr Wilf reached the top of the garden he was suddenly distracted when he noticed that someone was still bouncing on the bouncy castle. So he looked back to the tree to do a head count, and everyone was still there trying to coax the mischievous pair down from the tree, so who was on the bouncy castle, who could it be he thought? All he could see from the back of the bouncy castle was a head going up and down, but he couldn't make out who it was, and whoever it was they were wearing a hat!

Mr Wilf once again struck his Ninja pose and crept around the inflatable castle to have a peek, when he did he saw to his horror it was Chase Me Chase Me bouncing up and down with a demented grin on its face as though it hadn't a care in the world, bouncing like there was no tomorrow and it looked to be enjoying every second of it, and for some reason it was wearing Mr Wilf's best Sunday trilby and George's spare Bayern Munich football shirt too.

Mr Wilf stood there in amazement, he couldn't believe his eyes, he just stood watching in wonder as his invention was enjoying itself... that is until he was suddenly reminded by a shout from the bottom of the garden.

"Where's those stepladders Granddad?" yelled George and Charlie's dad. On hearing this Mr Wilf suddenly snapped out of his bewilderment and with a bit of sharp thinking and without hesitation he swiftly pulled out the plug for the bouncy castle blower and pushed the side walls in as it deflated, then quickly climbed on top ensuring that it collapsed down trapping Chase Me Chase Me inside. Then he quickly folded the bouncy castle up the best he could and put it back into the giant bag it had come in. But he had done it so fast he was now totally out of breath and exhausted, so he decided to sit down on top of this now very lumpy package to regain his wind for just a few moments. However these restful moments were short, when once again he was reminded by the same voice from the bottom of the garden shouting "Granddad where's them ladders, you better hurry up or all your apples will be eaten!"

"Oh dear," Mr Wilf gasped at the very thought, and quickly jumping to his feet he hurriedly set of down the garden, grabbing the stepladders on his way. The trouble was by the time he had got back to the tree where the steps were needed, he was so extraordinarily jiggered and out of breath, he was now glowing red in the face! On his family noticing this they all automatically assumed that their Granddad Wilf was having a bit of a funny turn, which made them all instantly rush to his aid.

"Here give me those ladders Granddad," his son demanded to lighten his burden, and before Mr Wilf knew it all his family members were helping to sit him down on the ground, each enquiring the same, "Are you ok Granddad?"

Charlie and George both seeing their Granddad's distress, climbed down the tree with no effort at all, (like the pair of little monkey's they really were), and came running over to his aid also enquiring the same, "Are you ok Granddad?" "Oh yes, I'm fine it's nothing," Mr Wilf replied, but all the while he was milking all the sudden attention as much as he could, hoping to divert it away from the bouncy castle that was no longer there.

Eventually after a lot of pampering and luckily for Mr Wilf, everyone else was soon in agreement that Granddad had overdone it and was in need of a lay down. Seeing as they were all tired too, they thought it was perhaps time for everyone to call it a day and go home so he could have his rest.

So that been settled everyone quickly gathered up their belongings and made their way to the front door and because they were all so concerned about Granddad, no one even noticed that the bouncy castle was missing!

Just as his family were about to leave and say their goodbyes, Mr Wilf was now so confident he had got away with concealing his invention from everyone else, his curiosity got the better of him when he asked little Charlie a question.

"Charlie can you tell me something, how on earth did you get up the tree by yourself", and to Mr Wilf's absolute horror Charlie surprised him, when he said,

"That Robot in your shed put me up there Granddad!"

Mr Wilf gulped, and before either of them could say another word, Charlie's dad had snatched Charlie up by his ankles, dangled him upside down and began tickling him.

"Come on you, bedtime" he said, thinking Charlie was just talking silly and although he was still trying his best to elaborate on his tale about this Robot, he couldn't for laughing so much, because Granddad was tickling him to make sure he couldn't continue on with his story. Luckily for Mr Wilf, Charlie was whisked away to the car still giggling and being tickled by his dad. Before anymore could be said, everyone had waved their goodbyes and the family cars had set off on their way home.

"Phew, that was a close shave" gasped Mr Wilf, and after shutting the door behind him, he began rubbing his hands together in anticipation of what he was about to do before returning to the very lumpy package he had to leave in so much of a hurry.

It was still there just as he had left it, so Mr Wilf knelt down beside it and put his ear near to have a listen inside and have a feel around with his hands for any sign of movement, but all was still, there was no sound or movement at all! Mr Wilf now felt confident enough to leave Chase Me Chase Me inside the bouncy castle until the morning, when he was more than sure its batteries would be definitely flat by then, and it couldn't present any more problems.

However, no sooner had he reached that conclusion, it also occurred to him at the same time that Chase Me Chase Me could have put little Charlie in the tree as a distraction so it could have a go on the bouncy castle and it must have been in the shed charging itself and watching them all of the time. With this extra thought in mind Mr Wilf took the added precaution of securing the bundle with some duct tape to make sure it couldn't get out and placed a wooden mallet near to hand, just in case it did.

That being sorted, all that was left to do was make a decision before going to bed, and being so very tired he made one quickly.

"Right then" he said to himself, to muster up a bit of an unnaturally stern voice "it's the end of the road for you tomorrow I'm afraid Chase Me Chase Me, you're too much trouble for me at my age." On that final note Mr Wilf turned off the patio lights and went back inside the house, where he made himself his usual mug of hot milk, but because he was so tired he skipped his pipe and went straight to bed and he was soon fast asleep, snoring till morning.

When Sunday morning came Mr Wilf had a full day of things to do, the first thing on his mind was Chase Me Chase Me, who was still inside the bouncy castle which had to be returned back to the Dog and Ferret that very day, and what to do with it when he got it out was also troubling him.

None the less Mr Wilf had a routine, the same routine every Sunday, which he would never break no matter what, so everything else would have to take second place.

Firstly, Mr Wilf went to the greenhouse to pick a nice bunch of flowers, then returning inside he put on his best tweed suit, combed his hair, tweaked his moustache to absolute perfection, then topped himself off with a nice fresh carnation on his lapel. But when he reached for his best trilby it wasn't there was it?

"Oh dear, oh dear," he muttered, "This won't do at all," and because he had to keep to his timetable he just picked up his flowers and went straight out of the door and set off to the cemetery regardless.

On his way there Mr Wilf just happened to spot the same group of naughty boys from the other night, and to his big surprise instead of being their usual scruffy selves they were all now dressed very smart and following them close behind were their parents in their Sunday best and it looked like they were herding their kids to Church.

"Well, well, well indeed, wonders will never cease," Mr Wilf muttered to himself, but at the same time making sure he covered his face with the bunch of flowers as he passed them by, not only to hide his face but also his huge gleeful grin. Just at that very moment Bill the landlord came out of the Dog and Ferret.

"Ho, hello Mr Wilf, have you done with the bouncy castle then" he enquired, and without a thought and still chuckling at the sight of those young boys going to church Mr Wilf replied, "Yes thank you very much," and before he was out of earshot, Bill added, "And will you be coming for your Sunday dinner as usual Mr Wilf?"

"Of course", replied Mr Wilf with a puzzled look on his face. "I wouldn't miss that for anything Bill, why do you ask?"

"Well," Bill smirked, "You're not wearing your best Sunday hat." To which they both instantly burst into laughter as though it was some kind of brilliant joke. They then parted company and went their separate ways, both still smiling at the big joke as they did.

It wasn't long before Mr Wilf concluded his business at the cemetery and was soon back at the Dog and Ferret tucking into his Sunday dinner, quaffing a milk stout, followed up by his favourite dessert – sticky toffee pudding.

Just as he was finishing off his dessert, Bill the landlord reminded him on passing the table, "Mr Wilf, my brother needs the bouncy castle by tea time, can he come by later and pick it up?" Mr Wilf was ever so grateful and accepted the offer without hesitation.

"Oh yes, yes that will save me a journey, thank you so very much indeed."

Mr Wilf was much happier now, and bearing in mind he still had that little job to do, the offer from Bill meant time wasn't pressing him now, so he decided to stay a little longer and have a few more ales in the pub.

After a few more ales, Mr Wilf bid everyone a

merry farewell with his usual cheery-bye and headed homeward bound.

The trouble was that by the time Mr Wilf had arrived home he was overcome with tiredness because he had eaten and drank far too much in the pub and now he was feeling very bloated and in desperate need of a little rest, so he thought it wise to perhaps have forty winks first and deal with his little problem outside later. After all it was still early and there was plenty of time left in the day and so that's what he did.

Four hundred winks later Mr Wilf eventually woke up and after a good old yawn and a stretch he glanced up at the mantlepiece clock, it was nearly tea time! He quickly jumped out of his rocking chair and went straight out of the back door onto the patio where he had left the bouncy castle, but to his horror it wasn't there, it had gone!

Mr Wilf was totally flabbergasted and he began scratching his head like he didn't know what to think or to do next, when all of a sudden the telephone rang, dering... dering...

"Oh dear, I don't like the sound of that," he said, and almost reluctantly he went to answer it regardless. When he picked it up his premonitions were only to prove right when he heard a very familiar voice at the other end that said, "Hello is that Mr Wilf?"

"Ho, hello," Mr Wilf replied, "Who is this?"

"It's Sgt Grimper here."

On hearing this voice Mr Wilf nearly dropped the phone, but nervously answered anyway.

"Yes, yes and what can I do for the police?" he enquired, while biting his fingernails.

"Aww it's not police business," said Sgt Grimper. "I'm just ringing to inform you I took the liberty of taking the bouncy castle from your garden for my daughter's birthday party. I saw you sleeping in your chair and didn't want to disturb you, is that alright?" he asked, adding, "Didn't my brother Bill tell you?"

"Oh yes, yes," a relieved Mr Wilf replied, but also nervously enquiring, "Err, err, Sgt Grimper, have you had chance to open up the package yet? As I didn't have time to check it over for you, and, and…"

"Oh no, that's alright," interrupted Sgt Grimper. "I'm sure it's fine."

"No, no," Mr Wilf insisted. "I would still like to come down and check it just in case."

"No… no, everything will be ok, no need" replied Sgt Grimper.

"But, but…" said Mr Wilf, trying to tell the sergeant what might be inside, however he was interrupted by Sgt Grimper once again.

"I turned on the blower just before I rang you Mr Wilf, and it looks like it's going up now, I can see it through the window."

"Oh dear," said Mr Wilf.

"Why, what's the matter Mr Wilf? The kids haven't had any accidents in it have they?"

"No... no," replied Mr Wilf. "I may have left something inside and I'm a bit worried." But before Mr Wilf could finish his sentence Sgt Grimper interrupted again.

"Mr Wilf don't you worry, I'll check it now" and before Mr Wilf could say another word Sgt Grimper had already put the phone down and gone.

Mr Wilf was now frantically beside himself with worry as to what might happen, he was biting his fingernails and tightly holding the phone to his ear listening intently for any sound from the other end, and all the while he was waiting he was expecting the worst.

"Oh dear, oh dear, what am I going to do, what am I going to do?" he kept repeating to himself, when all of a sudden he heard approaching footsteps towards the phone and Sgt Grimper picked it up again.

"Hello, Mr Wilf?"

"Yes, yes, I'm still here" a very nervous Mr Wilf answered.

"Well I certainly found out what you were so concerned about and had left in the bouncy castle Mr Wilf," said the sergeant, but now in a more policeman-detectivey-type of voice, only for Mr Wilf to now reply in a now much softer and ready to confess sort of voice.

"Oh dear Sergeant, what did you find?"

"Well, I found your property alright. I've got it here now."

"Here now?" blurted Mr Wilf, pulling at his collar to let some steam out.

"I've got it here in my hand."

"Here in your hand?" Mr Wilf repeated, who by this time was on the verge of having a heart attack, however it left him no choice but to ask what it was the sergeant had in his hand.

"And what is...." But before he could finish, the sergeant continued,

"Yes, I found your best Sunday trilby!"

On hearing this news Mr Wilf was so relieved he was half laughing and half crying, he just didn't know what think or say next, only then to hear Sgt Grimper go on further to say, "And I've found something else as well."

On hearing this Mr Wilf just gave up and was ready to hear the bad news.

"Yes Sergeant and what else may I ask have you found this time?" he said very calmly, all the while thinking he had found you know who....

"Well I found what looks like some kind of foreign football shirt to me, but I will fetch them over for you tomorrow, I've got a party to attend to, so bye bye Mr Wilf, got to go now" Then he just hung up!

On hearing this great news Mr Wilf dropped

the phone and just fell back into his chair in total relief, and let out the biggest sigh in the world.

"Thank goodness!" he gasped, but just as he sat back in his chair thinking everything was ok and he could finally relax, he suddenly realized something wasn't quite right, "Just a minute," he muttered, then realizing what it was, he jumped up out of the chair at least two foot off the ground and shouted out at the top of his voice in absolute frustration, "BUT WHAT HAPPENED TO CHASE ME CHASE ME?"

One Week Later

A Turn of Events

It was yet another day in the small town of Normantofts and there in his humble house on the edge of the wood Mr Wilf was up bright an early as usual getting ready for the special day ahead. Not only was he making preparation for his weekly routine, but also a very special event, Nana Morse's 150th birthday party. Nana was Mr Wilf's in-law from the opposite half of the family who had outlived all the other granddads and grandmas on her side and she was more commonly known by all who knew her as Nana Norser. She actually inherited her nickname on account that she used to tell everyone that her ancestors first arrived in the area by sailing up river in a longboat. But the real truth was that over the generations none of her grandkids could ever pronounce her name properly.

She was a little lady and wrinkled like a prune who resembled an old Tibetan woman from high up in the mountains. Her spine was so curved and bent she could only walk half stooped which made it look like she had a humped back. Despite her outward appearance she was a lovely kind old lady who was well respected and liked by almost everyone.

Today was Sunday and a very sunny day it was too when Mr Wilf set off on his usual visit to the cemetery. From there he planned to go straight on to Nana Norsers' birthday bash where he was expecting to meet half the town there, so as usual he was dressed and preened to perfection, especially his show stopping handlebar moustache because it was the national handlebar moustache competition this week, which he had won most years, so it was already in pre-competition condition.

As Mr Wilf neared the shops he began to notice lots of different people hanging about who were strangers in town. Not only that, there were also a few off-road vehicles with queer-looking aerials on their roofs and vans with what looked like satellite dishes on them too. A little further down the road he then saw some of these strangers walking about with weird devices that they were pointing in the air, which was also very strange? The first thing that popped into Mr Wilf's head was could it have anything to do with Chase Me Chase Me, but discounted that possibility almost straight away in the realization that it had been a week since that little escapade, and he had gone to great lengths searching for the Robot only to find no trace of it at all, and it definitely wouldn't be in the sky in any case, so what could it be, he thought?

Before he could come to any conclusion everything was made perfectly clear when Mr Wilf was approached by a bunch of people of a hippy type of appearance (anyone with long hair to Mr Wilf), who were handing out leaflets to passers-by. On receiving one he immediately perused its contents curious to know what it was all about. It read....

'TOWN MEETING to discuss the strange anomalies in Normantofts, lights in the woods and possible UFO activity in the area etc., 7 o'clock tonight, etc. etc.'

"NONSENSE, ABSOLUTE TWODDLE" snapped Mr Wilf, and screwing the leaflet up in his hand, he was just about to show his contempt by consigning it to the litter bin in full view of the people handing them out, when he heard,

"Pssssssssst, pssssssssssst, Mr Wilf, Mr Wilf... over here! Over here!"

On looking around to see where it came from, he spotted old Mr Snooby stood half hidden behind a large potted tropical plant in the town hall doorway and he was beckoning Mr Wilf towards him with his index finger. Mr Wilf stepped over towards Mr Snooby obligingly and also curious to see what he wanted.

"Whatever is the matter Mr Snooby?" he enquired,

"I told you... I told you all, didn't I Mr Wilf, they didn't believe me, but you do, don't you?" rambled Mr Snooby.

Not really wanting to encourage Mr Snooby too much, but still trying to remain polite, Mr Wilf replied "Now, now Mr Snooby of course I do, but let's keep it between me and you." Then he gave him the old 'mum's the word' gesture with his finger to his lips, followed by the obligatory nod and a wink. But as Mr Wilf was trying to part company and bid his usual farewell and leave him with that reply, Mr Snooby suddenly grabbed his arm and pulled him back closer toward him and whispered near his ear.

"The Aliens that are visiting now are getting things ready for a full invasion, just you wait, mark my words!"

Then after looking left and right to make sure no one else was about, he added,

"It was one of their reconnaissance drone Robots that kick me up the backside you know."

On hearing this absurdity Mr Wilf could hardly contain himself from bursting into laughter. However, still desperate to get a move on he decided to just humour him instead by making light of his warnings, "Well I don't know about all that Mr Snooby but I've got to admit something certainly put an end to your poaching antics didn't it now?!" And while Mr Snooby's brain was still engaged trying think of an answer, Mr Wilf used the opportunity to escape his grip and bid him his usual cheery-bye and continued on his way, but not without hearing Mr Snooby's parting words,

"I've seen it again, I've seen it again Mr Wilf!"

Although Mr Wilf heard what Mr Snooby had said, he showed it no concern at all, he just carried on his way to the cemetery regardless.

A little bit further up the road on passing the Dog and Ferret, Bill the landlord bobbed his head out the pub window and shouted to him from across the street, "Are you going to the do then" to which Mr Wilf only had to lift his hat up on his head two inches and back down again to indicate he was, but he was in a bit of a hurry, which Bill acknowledged by saying "See you there then".

No sooner had Mr Wilf placed his hat back on his head, he suddenly realized that he was still holding that silly leaflet about UFO's in his hand, noticing he had he couldn't help thinking about Mr Snooby and all his wild notions about Aliens and the response he got telling everyone in the pub. What really cracked him up was the fact that so called old Mr Snooby or Snubbers as they used to call him, was a year below him at school, and although it was completely out of character for the occasion, it made him laugh all the way to the cemetery.

A little later in the morning just after concluding his solemn duties, Mr Wilf decided that rather than go straight to Nana's party by travelling in style in a taxi, so he could look his very best on arrival as planned, he chose the alternative of taking a constitutional walk there instead.

This journey would take him along by the river downstream and passing by the old abandoned mine workings that were deep inside Spooker's Wood, before eventually ending up where Nanna lived, which just happened to be in one of only two houses in that area and her neighbour just happened to be a certain Sgt Grimper!

This was the real reason for Mr Wilf's sudden detour and extended journey, it was those parting words of old Mr Snooby "I've seen it again", that set him thinking and were still ringing in his ears. Even though he didn't let on to Mr Snooby at the time, it left him feeling a little bit uneasy, because although no one else took Mr Snooby seriously, Mr Wilf certainly did, especially about his encounters with Chase Me Chase Me anyway.

So to finally get peace of mind he had no other option than to get to the bottom of things to make sure his invention wasn't still running around on the loose and causing mischief, and perhaps being the real reason why all these UFO chasers were hanging about in the first place. So he decided to finally tie up all the loose ends by starting a search from where Chase Me Chase Me's last known location was?

Seeing as Mr Wilf had already combed the entire area around his own house last week and couldn't find any trace of him, the only other possible place left where Chase Me Chase Me could have got out of the bouncy castle was at Sgt Grimper's House.

The sergeant was more commonly known as 'the Grimp' by the criminal fraternity, because it was said that once he puts the Grimp on a suspect he never lets go until the case is solved. So now with that same determination Mr Wilf set off downstream on the riverbank to commence his long search while heading towards his intended destination, and leaving no stone unturned as he went.

Eventually, after taking longer than Mr Wilf had expected he finally arrived at the rear of Nana Norser's and the Grimp's houses. Unfortunately having searched all his way there he was still none the wiser to the whereabouts of his invention and now he was fed up of searching and ready to give it up completely and just regard Chase Me Chase Me as lost and missing in action. However before he could leave it at that, he thought he better check out one last thing first by taking a little peek into Sgt Grimper's back garden, which he did by standing on a pile of rubble that was dumped next to the rear wall. No sooner he did he spotted a bright yellow patch on the lawn, which was a good indication where the bouncy castle had been the week before. As he visually traced back to the nearest part of the wall to where it was sited, he also noticed that a couple of capstones had been dislodged from the top and were now lying on the ground. On checking this out he found to his horror that directly below the wall and next to the fallen capstone, and confirming his worst suspicions, there were big recognizable boot prints in the mud and they looked to be heading straight through the stream and deep into the woods.

"Oh deary me" gasped Mr Wilf, he didn't know what to do next, he had a real predicament on his hands now. Although he still had Nana Norser's special birthday party to attend and he could hear the festivities that sounded a lot of fun, his curiosity was getting the better of him, and now he wanted to follow the boot prints instead.

"What should I do, what should I do?" he asked himself. So to determine this he decided to consult his moustache by tweaking it at each end, as he always maintained that his moustache was the aerial for his brain which connected him to the cosmos and helped him in any big decision making.

However before he could he suddenly noticed that all the party music had stopped and then he heard what sounded like the guests singing the finishing chorus of happy birthday.

They sang, "Happy birthday dear great-great-great-grandma, happy birthday to you".

This was a big disappointment to Mr Wilf, it was like a double whammy punch to his gut, not only had he missed out on that special moment and the high point of Nanna's day, but now he had more problematic things to contend with as well. Although that being the case, on hearing what he had already missed out on, his mind was made up for him.

So he decided that because the day was still young he would have a little search for Chase Me Chase Me now, and go to Nana's birthday bash a bit later on. And so that's what he did.

Mr Wilf set off following the big boot prints tracking them wherever they went... at first the tracks went through the stream and then over to the other side, then back through the stream again, which continued for quite a while, forcing him to have to bob and weave his way through the thick undergrowth and paddle in the stream as he went.

After a while of this occurrence he came to the conclusion that these tracks were zigzagging purposely, as though to put someone off tracking them, it was certainly putting him off and by now he was getting tired and a bit disheveled too. His trousers were torn and he was soaked up to the knees, his jacket was thread-pulled by the dense thorny thicket, and unlike Chase Me Chase Me it seemed, Mr Wilf's batteries did begin to wear down, and rapidly too.

On spotting what looked like a nice clearing with a mound of grass which looked soft and dry to rest upon, he took the opportunity to sit for a while to gain his strength back. The trouble was, when he went to sit down... just as he was about to park his bum... this mound of grass jumped up and started shouting,

"Hey what do you think you're doing... what's your game pal?

It wasn't a pile of grass at all, it was a man dressed in a grassy camouflage outfit (ghillie suit) and carrying a camera too.

Mr Wilf nearly jumped out of his skin with fright

"What on earth are you doing down there?" he demanded at the top of his voice to the camouflaged man, and to Mr Wilf's amazement the Cammo man equally demanded to know the same in return

"Never mind what I'm doing, what do you think you're up to..." he said

"I was just having a sit down," replied Mr Wilf. "Well I've been watching you," retaliated the Cammo man. "I've been watching you hopping and jumping about in the stream like a mad man, what's all that about then?" Cammo man demanded

"Well errr... It's a new old age sport that keeps ya fit, don't ya know?" replied Mr Wilf, then purposely reversing the conversation, he added

"Never mind that, what's your game then?"

"Aliens," the Cammo guy quickly replied. "Some say they are seen coming from down there," he said, pointing to an old mine entrance hidden in the trees.

"Nonsense," rebuked Mr Wilf trying to change the subject quickly. "Haven't you got better things to do than going around scaring people dressed like the creature from the Black Lagoon... it ought to be a crime it did!" Only to hear a now angry Cammo man blast in a disgruntled complaining manner, "I've nowt better to do now have I... now you've blown my cover? I've been here five hours," he moaned.

In that instant Cammo man then began hurriedly collecting up all of his gear, and once he had he suddenly marched off stomping down the path towards the town.

Seeing that he had Mr Wilf decided to stick around for a while, and after double-checking that Cammo man had actually gone, and inspired by what he had just heard him say about the Aliens in the mine – Mr Wilf couldn't resist checking it out for himself, and because he didn't believe in Aliens, it meant that the only other thing that could be down there had to be Chase Me Chase Me didn't it?

So Mr Wilf wasted no time making his way

toward the old mine entrance, but treading very carefully as he went too, because the ground was uneven under foot, loose rocks were everywhere and the path was overgrown with saplings and bushes all the way.

When he finally reached what looked like the mine entrance he noticed an old sign that was hanging down from a post by a length of rusty barbed wire. It read

'DANGER DEEP MINE WORKINGS, KEEP OUT!' After reading this and nearing the edge of this dangerous chasm Mr Wilf decided as a precaution to get down on his hands and knees and crawl the rest of the way, not only for safety, but also to surprise what might be down there.

On all fours he crept silently towards this great hole in the ground, all the while being very careful not to make a sound. When he eventually reached the edge he cautiously poked his head over the top of the hole and peered down.

To his huge surprise it wasn't very deep at all! It had been mostly filled in and only looked about thirty feet deep, that one could easily scale down it, if not walk down, thought Mr Wilf.

So that's exactly what he did. Firstly he began by grasping a hold of the creeper vines that were hanging over the side to steady his way, using them like a rope he slowly began descending backwards, steadily walking step by step towards the bottom. As he did and seeing that the hole was already shaded by the trees, it got much darker the deeper he went, so in desperation to see where he was going Mr Wilf held the vines with one hand then searched his waistcoat for his trusty lucky thumb-buster lighter to light the way.

Unfortunately on finding it, and trying to hold on with one hand and strike his lighter up with the other, he lost his footing and then the grip with his other hand and suddenly fell backwards down the hole.

"WHAAAAAAAAAAAAAAA" wailed Mr Wilf as he went tumbling head over heels backwards down the hole and hit the bottom like a big sack of spuds. Fortunately he landed in a big pile of dead leaves and undergrowth which cushioned his impact on landing. There was dust and dead leaves flying everywhere, even the resident bats decided enough was enough and flew outside for a breath of fresh air.

When the dust eventually settled, a stunned and dazed Mr Wilf managed to sit upright and give himself a quick check over. Miraculously he found that he was not only totally unscathed and ok, but what was even more surprising he was still clutching his lucky thumb-buster lighter in his hand, which he wasted no time in striking it up to see where he was... but more importantly, to see who or what might be down there with him.

When he held his lighter aloft it illuminated the whole cave, and on quickly looking around the very first thing he noticed was... it was completely empty, there were definitely no Aliens down there. To make sure he shuffled around on his bum to look in the opposite direction with his thumb buster to see if there was any trace of his Robot at all, but when he did he suddenly felt something hard in the pile of dead leaves he was sitting on, so after scooching over a bit on one cheek to feel around, he felt a heavy metal object and after pulling it out and brushing off the debris, it revealed an old-style shotgun with its barrel bent backwards and out of shape, and that's not all, from the direction he was now sat he also noticed what looked like a small hollow or deep crack in the side of the rock. So again using his lucky thumb buster lighter to light his way he cautiously crawled over to investigate what might be in there.

To his surprise when he peered inside he saw that it was full of strange little parcels and boxes with labels on. On picking one up and on further inspection, to Mr Wilfs astonishment he saw they all had his name and address on them. They were all his spare parts from out of his shed and some of his tools were there too, but where was Chase Me Chase Me he thought? After checking once again that he was still indeed on his own, Mr Wilf decided to just sit there for a while to recover from his tumble, but also to utilise his time there to try and figure everything out what was going on?

All the while he sat there figuring he was starting to think very differently about his invention, and the more he thought about it the more he began to wonder what he had actually built. So he began searching his memory to try and find that out, ironically though, he must have forgotten to top up his thumb buster lighter, because it began to flicker and within only a few seconds... it went out.

Leaving Mr Wilf now sat down a big deep hole in the middle of the woods all alone and in the dark! None the less he just sat there still pondering what to do about his invention.

He wasn't that long in his pondering though, when his concentration was suddenly interrupted by the sound of movement coming from the top of the hole. On quickly glancing upwardly he caught a fleeting glimpse of a shadow that crossed the beam of daylight that was shining down. Noticing this he wasted no time jumping to his feet and immediately began to scramble up the steep rocky incline as fast as he could, by using the creeper vines in the way he was supposed to have come down, huffing and puffing towards daylight he climbed.

It was much harder than he expected, and by

the time he neared the top he was exhausted and totally out of breath, yet still determined to see who it was that made the shadow, he somehow managed to summon up enough energy to stealthily spring to his feet to try to surprise who ever it was. On a quick scan of the immediate area and hoping to see Chase Me Chase Me standing there to greet him, he was only to be disappointed to see the white rear end of a startled Roe Deer disappearing into the dense thicket instead.

So after that pleasant disappointment, a now very tired and disheveled Mr Wilf decided it was best to turn in his search for the day and make his way back to Nana Norser's to attend her birthday bash as planned.

The trouble was he had spent that much time searching it was now getting late and he really needed to make tracks back to Nana's as quick as he could. So he began tidying and brushing himself down as he went the long arduous way that he came.

Quite sometime later Mr Wilf eventually arrived back at Nana Norser's rear garden gate where he paused for a few moments to compose himself before entering, and realizing that it was a bit late and he had missed out on most of the special day, he couldn't make the grand entrance he normally did on these type of occasions. So instead he decided that he would try to sneak into the party without drawing to much attention to himself. Unfortunately though, on peeking through a knot-hole in the fence he saw he was out of luck, almost everyone had gone home and there weren't enough people left to mingle in with, which meant he would stand out like a sore thumb.

So as an alternative Mr Wilf thought he would make light of his late appearance by doing something different and turn his belated arrival into some kind of fun.

He took a deep breath and after the count of three, he suddenly went bursting through the back gate into the garden where the remaining guests were sat, and shouted as loud as he could "TADAAAAA," to startle everyone.

However to his surprise he didn't get the reaction he was expecting, all of the remaining guests just burst into laughter instead, especially his grandchildren who excitedly came running over to welcome their Granddad Wilf, but they were pointing and laughing at him at the same time.

"Where have you been Granddad hahaha?" they all gigglingly enquired. Which was a total puzzlement to Mr Wilf, especially when he noticed that practically everyone else was doing the same pointing and laughing too.

That is until he saw his own reflection in the patio window and seeing what looked like a hobo staring back at him, he realized the joke was about his appearance. So Mr Wilf had no other choice but to make a joke of it too and join in the laughter as well, but all the while still trying to think of an excuse to explain why he was late for the party, where he had been and why he now looked like a tramp.

The problem was that before he could think up an alternative excuse, rather than tell everyone what he had really been up to (he didn't want to divulge he had been searching for his rogue invention in an old abandoned mine shaft), his grandson George posed those very same questions.

"Granddad, where have you been and why are you in fancy dress?" Which really put his Granddad on the spot now because it got all the other guest's immediate attention and they were keen to know the same too.

Now with all eyes focused on Mr Wilf, he took a big gulp and said the first thing that came into his head.

"I got lost in Spooker's Wood following deer tracks if you want to know."

And before he could think up an answer as to why, his smarty-pants grandson once again grabbing everyone's attention demanded to know that very answer too.

"Why Granddad" he asked, and because Granddad Wilf hadn't thought up an answer to that himself yet, he purposely began stuttering and stalling for time.

"Errrrr, to see where, where, where..." Only

then to come with the simplest answer of all.

"To see where they went don't ya know!"

To Mr Wilf's surprise this simple reply went down like a brilliant joke, which made everyone cry out with laughter, further adding to the whole comedy spectacle of Mr Wilf who was normally the smartest man in the village but now looked like a tramp.

Although all the fun was at Mr Wilf's expense at the moment, it was also to his advantage and a welcome distraction to what he had actually been up to.

Mr Wilf just played along with the jokes and before anyone else could make any further comments about his whereabouts or crack another joke about him being one of those UFO hunters, Nana Norser saved the day by making her grand appearance from the direction of the house on her mobility scooter, loudly interrupting everyone as usual with her familiar greeting.

"Hoy, hoy Mr Wilfers, where ya bin?" she yelled excitedly.

Nana Norser had until now been sat very quietly parked on the patio listening to everything and squinting her eyes.

You see, Nana Norser had the strangest selective hearing, she was often heard to say she couldn't see for listening because she always squinted her eyes to listen.

"Come here ya big pussycat," demanded Nana, "Give old grandma a kiss and a tickle with your big whiskers my Mr Wilfers."

This was an invitation Wilfers couldn't resist and with outstretched arms he eagerly went to give Nana Norser the biggest hug in the world. It was a sight so endearing to all and the laughter at Mr Wilf's expense was instantly replaced by awwwwws of admiration instead.

However those awwwwws soon transmogrified back into laughter again, but this time in Nana Norser's direction, on everyone overhearing her whisper loudly in his ear, while wearing a look of concern on her face.

"Isn't it about time you bought a new suit Wilfers, you're starting to look a bit scruffy of late."

This was a typical misunderstanding of Nana's but a very funny one none the less. Now with all focus back in Nana's direction, all attention and conversations soon returned back to everything about Nana and her special day. Once again things were back to normal and Mr Wilf could now finally relax. Well, for a little while anyhow.

Another Turn of Events

A little later on in the evening when only a few of the close family were still around, they were all seated in and around the conservatory part of the house. The adults were chatting away amongst themselves and the kids were all sat around their Granddad Wilf still poking fun at his appearance, thinking he had purposely come dressed as hobo, and laughing at the sight of his scraggy moustache because they had never seen it so disheveled before. Everyone was pretty much settled down and enjoying each other's company and the mood was a happy one.

When all of a sudden an item came on the local TV news which got everyone's immediate attention, because it was about Normantofts and it featured a TV presenter who was just announcing that the town was now officially the number one UFO hotspot in the UK. There in the TV studio were some of the people Mr Wilf had seen handing out the leaflets in the town earlier in the day.

These people who Mr Wilf had considered hippies were now in front of the camera and they were appealing for investigations to be made about some of the strange goings on in Spooker's

Wood. The police were also present, and they were saying that they were now considering sealing the town off to get to the bottom of it all, but mainly to deter hoaxers and trespassing on private land.

Hearing this news, there was simultaneous loud cry of "WHAT!" from just about everyone in the room, followed by a mad scramble for the TV remote to turn the volume up in disbelief. Then just at that moment the news item flashed to a live scene featuring another lady presenter who was actually standing outside the Town Hall in Normantofts, and she was talking about the many sightings of strange coloured lights which had been seen in and around Spooker's Wood at night. She also went on to report of an eye witness account of flying disc objects that had also been seen landing there, and as the camera panned to the right to reveal the actual eye witness standing next to her ready to be interviewed live on air, you'll never guess who it was? It was only old Mr Snooby.

"POPPYCOCK," Mr Wilf blasted loudly, jumping to his feet in frustration, "Flying discs indeed, it's that Mr Snooby making things up I tell you."

But before he could finish his rant, little Charlie interrupted with his understanding of things.

"It isn't Aliens Granddad, it's Chase M..." but before he could get another word out of his mouth he was quickly stopped by a sudden elbow nudge from his big brother George who was sitting by his side, who then followed up by quickly putting his hand over Charlie's mouth to shut him up and muffle what he was trying to say.

This didn't go unnoticed by Granddad, who was very surprised, because he wasn't expecting that subject coming up at all, but he was more surprised to hear what Nana had to say when she piped up, adding to what perhaps Charlie was going to say.

"It's that Robot thing again, the kids play with him down't beck they do, he turned up last week he did, comes int garden he does."

Mr Wilf was speechless on hearing this revelation, but on looking around for everyone's reaction, he saw that no one else in the room had taken a blind bit of notice of anything Nana had just said. They either didn't hear her or they thought it was just another one of Nana Norser's weird statements she came out with on a regular basis.

It was more than likely they were just too interested in watching the local topic on TV, he concluded.

Even so, Mr Wilf had taken notice of what Nana had said, and he was just about to tweak both ends of his moustache to try and figure things out, when he noticed that while almost everyone else was still glued to the TV, George, Charlie, Evie and even little Molly, who had obviously heard what Nana said about a Robot, were all now sat arms folded, wearing a frown and giving Granddad Wilf a certain 'we know a secret' type of stare instead.

Hmmmm, Granddad Wilf thought to himself, and in that instant he returned a 'I know you know something, but what? sort of stare back at them.

Then he lost all concentration again, when there was a call for quiet, followed by a chorus of shushes from the whole room.

"Shhhhh" everyone demanded, it was time for Mr Snooby to make his debut appearance on live TV. He was now stood in front of the camera and after being prompted by the presenter he went on to introduce himself and tell his story about the Aliens that had landed in Spooker's wood. He gave a full and in-depth account and a vivid description of his experience. At first he came across as a very believable witness with a plausible story, that is until the interviewer brought up Mr Snooby's other encounter which he probably hadn't really elaborated on to the interviewer beforehand, but he told his tale regardless.

"Well I was in Spooker's Wood late one afternoon and I was trying to shoot a bit of something for mi supper." Mr Snooby then paused for a moment and nervously pulled his collar at the same time (probably having realized he had just admitted to poaching on live TV). So now a more nervous and less confident looking Mr Snooby went on to tell his story.

"Where was I...? Oh I know... when this Robot thing came up from behind me and kicked me up the backside!"

Hearing what Mr Snooby just said and before he could go on the interviewer grabbed the microphone and pulled it away from him as quick as she could and was trying to end the interview on that note, but the trouble was Mr Snooby wanted to continue with his tale. He swiftly yanked the microphone back and despite the news presenter still pulling on the cable wire at the other end, and all much to the amusement of the spectators who were now in hysterics, as an insistent Mr Snooby somehow managed to keep ahold of it and struggle on with his story.

"It kicked me up the arse and I went flying through the air and down into this big deep hole, and when I managed to climb out the Alien took my gun and bent it around a tree."

Whatever he said after that didn't matter, it couldn't be heard for the uproar of laughter, not only from the crowd at the scene but also from the laughter inside Nana Norser's house where everyone was in absolute hysterics.

Surprisingly the loudest laughter wasn't coming from Mr Wilf who was known for his loud booming laugh, and although he was doing his best even shaking the chandelier, it was coming from Sgt Grimper's house next-door who must have also witnessed Mr Snooby's very own confession to poaching on live TV, not to mention all the other mad stuff about Aliens and Robots and such like.

Nana was having a whale of a time.

"It's the best I've heard in years," she cried as she rolled back and forth with laughter. Unfortunately in her over excitement and giddiness, she suddenly lost her balance and rolled back too far in her seat. This caused her to drop the finely rolled Cuban cigar she got for her birthday right onto her best Persian carpet, and on quickly trying to catch it before it burnt a hole in her precious rug she accidentally caught the accelerator lever on her mobility chair, making it set off suddenly speeding out of control with Nana barely clinging on one handed and riding side saddle, she went flying full throttle straight into the brand new 50-inch smart flat screen TV that everyone was watching, knocking it clean off its stand and sending it crashing to the floor, which made a really loud bang accompanied with a blue flash of light, followed by an almost perfect mushroom cloud of white smoke rising up to the ceiling.

It was so funny the kids began to clap as though it was some carefully crafted piece of pantomime, while everyone else were either on the floor kicking their legs in the air like upturned beetle's or just holding their ribs crying with laughter. Despite the enormity of damage caused by Nana's demolition derby and the sad fact they no longer had a TV to watch, it was still the best finale to end a day's entertainment at Nana Norser's house ever.

When the smoke had eventually cleared and everyone was too belly sore to laugh any more, and Nana Norser's whisky bottle, which she was given to calm her down was eventually prized from her fingers, everybody decided to pitch in to clear away all the mess and tidy up for Nana before going home.

By the time everything was done and made spic and span, everyone was really tired and more than ready for bed. Although that being the case, when it came time for everyone to get their coats and ready to say their goodbyes to their Nana and each other, Granddad Wilf surprised everyone when he suddenly declined all offers of a lift home in the car. To everyone's astonishment he then mysteriously announced that he was going to walk home through the woods (The very same woods he admitted getting lost in earlier) to take in the night air instead.

At first no one took him seriously, they just laughed it off and thought he was having a big joke, that is until he asked to borrow a torch to light his way from Nana. No matter how much his family tried to talk him out of it, his mind was made up and that's what he was going to do.

So after that being settled, Mr Wilf and his family parted company in Nana's hallway, they went waving their goodbyes through the front door and Mr Wilf bid his usual cheery bye and went out the back.

It was in the light of all this new information that made Mr Wilf decide to get to the bottom of what was going on once and for all, especially after what he heard Nana say about the Robot earlier, not to mention the secretive behavior of his grandkids as well, which was a very good indication that they knew more than he did, but now he was hoping to change that situation, so off into the darkness of Spooker's Wood again he went.

All the way home he was scanning every shadow, every noise he heard he quickly shone his light hoping to catch site of his invention and each time he did he wasn't sure what to expect. Was it Chase Me Chase Me or was it just another encounter with the likes of Cammo man again he thought.

The further on he went he kept hearing one noise after another. One such noise turned out to be a fox and a couple of its cubs scurrying away. Then he saw two large eyes glaring at him from out of the trees, which was a bit unnerving but it turned out to be a tawny owl that hooted at him when it was caught in his light, to which Mr Wilf couldn't resist hooting back. He also heard the deer deep in the wood rubbing their horns against the trees.

But then, a little further along the path nearer towards home, the night suddenly went dead quiet and very still. That's not all, the hairs began to prickle up on the back of his neck, which was the usual feeling he got when he thought he was being watched. As a precaution he decided to duck for cover and creep quietly on his tiptoes in an attempt to surprise whoever or whatever it might be.

When all of a sudden he then began to hear voices coming from the bushes in front of him, so he stayed still for a few moments to listen. He then heard what sounded like people talking on a two-way radio and they seemed very close by too. So he slowly crept forward a little nearer to find out who it was, when he heard a radio voice say,

"Copy that, I have a Foxtrot Alpha Tango... Bravo Lima Oscar Kilo Echo... Oscar November... Papa Alpha Tango Hotel... over."

Hearing this and understanding the phonetic alphabet, Mr Wilf reacted abruptly and retaliated by shouting in the direction he thought the radio voices were coming from, "I HOPE YOUR'E NOT REFERRING TO ME WHOEVER YOU ARE!" and then quickly shone his light in the same direction. He was just in time to catch in his beam of light what looked like another of the UFO fraternity shamefully retreating back into the undergrowth with his tail between his legs, but not before hearing Mr Wilf further boom his displeasure, "IT'S ABOUT TIME YOU LOT FOUND A JOB," and likewise it wasn't without Mr Wilf hearing the reply he got either, when a voice shouted back, but from a different direction in the dark, "IT IS OUR JOB," the voice said, which Mr Wilf thought was very funny and he couldn't help but laugh out loud right there on the spot, nor could he resist returning the comment.

"Sir, I don't know who you are, but the very idea and absurdity of this indeed being a job is what's wrong with this country today," he rebuked, only to hear a disgruntled sneer from one direction and a "Whatever" from another. This only instigated Mr Wilf to reply in astonishment "My God, how many are you?"

Having had his say and despite how amusing the situation was, Mr Wilf decided it was better to part company with the Alien hunters, happy in the knowledge that these types of folk were usually quite harmless and just a bunch of weirdo's who liked rolling about in the undergrowth playing soldiers at night.

Although that being the case, it also occurred to him that after having this noisy exchange of words with this lot he had inadvertently advertised to the whole world his presence in the woods, to which he concluded that his efforts to surprise Chase Me Chase Me were now dashed and it was best just to make his way home as planned.

None the less he kept his eyes peeled and his ears pricked just in case. All the way back he neither saw or heard another thing, not one trace of his invention at all, which wasn't too surprising considering the amount of UFO hunters that were still lurking about in the woods at night, but he hoped that by tomorrow when the word got around about Mr Snooby's grand TV appearance, they might not be around much longer.

By the time Mr Wilf had reached the back yard of his house he had come to the opinion his journey had been a total waste of time and he was now too tired to even think about Chase Me Chase Me anymore, and all that was on his mind now was bedtime!

However on entering his rear garden gate he found that it was slightly ajar, although he definitely remembered shutting it tight earlier in the day. So as a precaution he had a quick scan around with his torch to see if anything else was amiss, and when he did to his huge surprise he could clearly see that there were big boot prints all over the ground.

Mr Wilf's heart instantly began racing in his chest, he turned off his torch and then very slowly opened the gate. No sooner it was open wide he quickly turned on his torch and shone a beam of light... but there was no one there. Be that as it may, when he scanned further up the garden and towards his house, he saw even more big boot prints, and they were leading right up to his shed.

Noticing this he quickly turned off his torch again and struck his usual Ninja pose, and using the cover of darkness he crept silently up the garden path and towards his shed. The first thing he noticed was that the shed door was closed, but the nearer he got and on closer inspection, he could see that the hinges had been unscrewed and that the door was only sat in place and just hanging on by the catch.

So Mr Wilf crept quietly up to the side of the shed where there was a window and he could have a look inside. Although it was dark the full moon provided a bit of light, but the only place he could see was the area of shelves where he stored things. Which just happened to be where he used to keep his spare parts, but ironically now only empty spaces remained, (because they were all down in the old mine). The rest of the shed was in darkness and he couldn't see in the dark corners at all, and although he couldn't Mr Wilf was now convinced that Chase Me Chase Me was in there somewhere. So he decided to squat down below the window to have a quick think, and within a flash he had come up with a plan.

He got his torch at the ready, then he began giving himself a starting countdown, "Five, four, three, two..." and on one, he jumped to his feet as quick as he could, with the torch held at the side of his head he immediately pressed his face up against the glass to see inside... only to get the fright of his life!

"Arrrrgh" Mr Wilf screamed, virtually jumping out of his shoes as he did, throwing his arms and torch up in the air in sheer fright...! He had only come face to face, eyeball to eyeball with Chase Me Chase Me, who was on the opposite side of the glass doing exactly the same, looking back at him and scaring him half to death in the process.

Mr Wilf leapt back in so much panic he accidentally stood on the garden rake with his heel, causing it's handle to rise up sharply and conk him at the back of his head. It gave him such a clout Mr Wilf let out a big "OOOPH", his legs suddenly buckled and his knees then knocked together before he slowly corkscrewed down to the ground, finally disappearing into the huge forest of rhubarb that was growing at the side of his shed. No sooner Mr Wilf's backside had hit the ground he heard a sudden loud thump which sounded like a shed door being booted from its hinges, followed by a very familiar Robot voice that said, "Cheery-bye Mr Wilfers... tickle me later... drop by at mine sometime why don't ya"

By the time Mr Wilf had crawled out from between the giant stalks of his prize-winning rhubarb and got to his feet, he only managed to catch the repeat performance of Chase Me Chase Me clearing the six foot garden fence with ease and disappearing in the direction of Spooker's wood.

Once again Mr Wilf found himself stood scratching his head in disbelief not knowing what to think or do next, but the truth was he was now too tired and too low on energy to do anything at all! So he just shrugged his shoulders and went inside the house where he could rest up and at least try to figure things out in comfort, which he needed to do before going to bed, because he could never sleep with things on his mind. After making his usual hot mug of milk and stoking up his tobacco pipe he sat in his rocking chair to ponder. There he sat rocking and blowing smoke rings in the air, tweaking his moustache at both ends in deep thought. Fortunately in only a short time of tweaking he had the eureka moment he was searching for and came up with another brilliant idea that he needed. With his mind now settled on what to do he finished off his milk and went straight to bed, in no time at all he was snoring till morning.

Epiphany

The next morning came fast as it usually does when you've had a really good sleep, and as usual Mr Wilf was up bright and early eating his pop tarts crunching away and thinking about the things he had to do that day. The first job that came to mind was making preparations for tomorrow night's annual handlebar moustache competition in Leeds, and although it was very important, he still had more pressing things that needed to be sorted out first, and that being Chase Me Chase Me.

After breakfast he went out into the garden where he immediately began pulling out lengths of old iron railings from behind his greenhouse and dragging them off and into his shed. When he had got all that he needed, he went inside and closed the door behind him. There he stayed, hammering and sawing, welding and grinding parts for the biggest part of the day.

It was around teatime when all the noises ceased and Mr Wilf finally emerged from his shed and leaving the door wide open behind him, he stood a while to admire his handiwork. He had constructed a steel cage inside his shed with a spring-loaded door which when triggered snapped shut on entry, trapping who or whatever came inside. Just to finish it off he had also installed an old railway signal on the outside of the shed that went to the up position to indicate when the trap was full.

So the trap was set and Mr Wilf was ready, all that was left to do now was wait!

And wait he did, not for one moment did he take an eye off the railway signal, not even while cooking his tea, he kept one eye on the shed and the other on his fish fingers. Teatime came and went and the minutes soon turned into hours in the waiting.

So now with plenty of time on his hands, Mr Wilf decided he might as well get comfortable. Which he did by sitting in his faithful rocking chair, but still careful to remain in full view of the shed and the train signal. The while he sat there he couldn't help thinking about the past events, all the mad stuff that had taken place since his little prank and all the fun he'd had, but also about the ridiculous situation he found himself in at that very moment in time. Not to mention the fright Chase Me Chase Me gave him last night, he would never have imagined things turning out the way they had. He thought his experiences were so funny they might even make a good children's story, well up to now anyway, as he was sure no harm had been caused so far and only been for the good as far as he could see.

But he still needed to get Chase Me Chase Me out of the picture for a while, hopefully then Normantofts could return to normal and no one would be any the wiser, and perhaps he might find out what made his invention tick in the first place, and how the Robot had been able to do what it had done up until now, and that's what Mr Wilf was more interested in finding out. It was certainly his main priority now.

With his mind settled on what he had to do, all that was left to do now was wait, but the sheer boredom was sending him to sleep, so to combat this Mr Wilf decided to keep himself occupied by going for a mooch around his garden to check things over.

Firstly he went to check his trap over, and it was still set and ready, then he checked the back garden gate, which was still shut tight but not bolted and everything was ok. However, on his way back up the garden path he spotted one of the little spare part parcels laying in his vegetable patch, which he assumed Chase Me Chase Me must have dropped while running out of the garden the night before or maybe on one of his other visits.

On picking it up he quickly opened the parcel curious to see what was inside.

It was a power cell, and it was the same type and from the same batch he had installed in his invention, but when he removed it from out of its packaging it felt slimy to the touch. On inspection he noticed it was covered in a veiny white mould that looked to be coming from out of a small corrosion spot where the wires went inside. It was also leaking some kind of White Goo stuff, which Mr Wilf couldn't help notice was glowing in the dark, and that's not all, he had now got it all over his hands and they were glowing too.

All of a sudden Mr Wilf began to feel really strange and he became a bit wobbly and unsteady on his feet, then lots of images went flashing through his mind, which at first didn't make any sense to him at all. In an instant his mood suddenly changed to feelings of wellbeing and extreme happiness and in those moments he then felt he could understand anything and everything he put his mind to, inventions, math problems, the true meaning of life, it was fantastic!

No matter how nice those feeling were though, Mr Wilf was a wise man who had been around the world a bit, and he had the good common sense to be aware that he could be suffering the hallucinogenic effects of some kind of poisoning from the White Goo substance. Realizing this he quickly snapped out of his euphoric state and urgently ran over to the greenhouse, where he plunged his hands straight into the giant water butt and began vigorously scrubbing the substance off his hands as quick as he could.

Fortunately, within only a few seconds of doing so he began to feel his usual self again.

"Phew, that was a close shave" he gasped, but an experience that had now left Mr Wilf even more curious than ever, and now he really needed to know what this Goo actually was and where it came from. After further inspection of the packaging and being careful not to get anymore on his skin, he noticed it was half-eaten by mould, to which he assumed was caused by the dampness in the shed that came from an over-flowing bottle garden which he had put in there years ago to catch a leak.

Mr Wilf also took into consideration that because the bottle was full of a whole host of different living organisms, perhaps this was the source of some kind, and as he had never heard of mould coming from a battery before, the only alternative explanation there could be was that the Goo must have come from the bottle garden.

Maybe it could have had something to do with the Robot's malfunction, was it the Goo? he thought.

After all this thinking Mr Wilf became more perplexed than ever, he just didn't know what to think anymore. He was even beginning to doubt his own judgment, because he had changed his mind so many times in the past week already. Firstly, when after his initial prank he decided to dismantle Chase Me Chase Me, then later he changed his mind again when he thought it was perhaps better to just change Chase Me Chase Me's appearance and reprogram him to do useful jobs about the garden or house or something, but since his Robot seems to have got his own intelligence from somewhere, what does he do now? Should he still try to dismantle him? Have I got a right to dismantle him? And mores' the question, would he let me? (Mr Wilf was now resigned to the fact that his invention was not only intelligent but may also be alive, so he began to refer to Chase Me Chase Me as a he now).

All of these questions were irrelevant at the moment, Mr Wilf still had to catch the dammed thing first, and perhaps then he might get all the answers, but until then his main priority was just to get Chase Me Chase Me out of the way for a while to finally put an end to all of this UFO nonsense and then Normantofts could return to normal, he hoped.

After returning the package to his shed Mr Wilf went back indoors and sat back in the rocking chair to resume his vigil from there, but by this time, because he had endured another long hard stressful day, he was soon overcome by tiredness. The longer he sat just watching and waiting the more tired he became and his eyelids got heavier and heavier until he could hardly keep his eyes open at all. At one stage he even tried watching with one eye at a time giving each a rest in turn, but it was no use, both eyes kept closing. To remedy this situation he came up with another brilliant idea! This was to tie a piece of string around the shed door handle and the other end to his big toe while he was sitting in his rocking chair, on the reckoning that if someone or something opened the shed door it would tug on his toe and wake him up if he fell asleep.

Seeing as he had a ball of string handy, he did just that. So now reassured by his trusty piece of string, Mr Wilf felt confident enough to dare to have forty winks. He made himself comfortable in the chair and put his bare feet on the kitchen table, and with his big toe pointing outside, he pulled the string taut and tied it on, then he laid back into his rocker to rest. Within less than a few minutes he was already snoring his head off in the deeeeepest of sleeps.

There he lay with the back door wide open with his big toe pointing into the dark of night snoring away the hours, and the while he slept he was totally unaware of all the visitors that came and went. He missed seeing a clan of badgers that ambled inside his kitchen to finish off his packet of biscuits and the milk he left at the foot of his chair. He didn't even notice the early morning robin that flew in for a nosey and landed on his head, nor the crafty weasel's that had a good look around inside Mr Wilf's shoes and played with one of his socks, he was aware of none.

As the morning light came Mr Golding the milkman came rattling down the path to deliver the milk. He was just putting down a bottle of semi-skimmed when he noticed this piece of string in his way, but when he pulled it to one side to pick up the empties he inadvertently tugged on Mr Wilf's big toe! Mr Wilf leapt out of his chair, but still half asleep he grabbed his walking stick and went running out the door shouting, "I GOT YA...I GOT YA NOW."

Mr Golding (or Goldy as he was locally known), was so startled by Mr Wilf's sudden appearance bursting out of the house waving his walking stick, he jumped to his feet and set off running as fast as he could down the garden path in absolute panic. So much so, he discarded his empties over his shoulder and climbed over the fence instead of using the gate. He wasn't hanging around for anyone.

Realizing his mistake and it wasn't who he thought it was, Mr Wilf began to shout for Goldy to come back.

"HOY, GOLDY... COME BACK, COME BACK. IT WAS A MISTAKE. YOU DON'T UNDERSTAND. I THOUGHT YOU WERE A ROBOT."

As one can imagine on Goldy hearing this it

was no surprise he didn't come back.

So Mr Wilf just shrugged his shoulders and decided that seeing as he was in the garden he might as well check his trap over while he was there. After careful inspection he found that everything was just as he left it, nonetheless it was still empty! So he untied his big toe and shuffled barefoot back into the kitchen to begin making breakfast as he normally did. Noticing the time and realizing he was up earlier than usual he thought it might be a good idea to accept Chase Me Chase Me's invitation, after all he did say, "drop by mine sometime why don't ya".

So after he had polished off his full English breakfast he put on his boots and went to get a length of rope from the garage, he then took the nets from George's practice goalposts and after he grabbed the flashlight from the kitchen cupboard, he loaded everything up in his wheelbarrow, and when he was sure he got what he needed he then set off through the back gate towards Spooker's Wood.

Arriving at his destination at the old abandoned mine Mr Wilf was so very careful to tread lightly from there on, so not to be heard. On nearing the mine he was parting the branches ever so slightly as he went, and when he was near the entrance, he got down on all fours and crept ever so quietly towards the edge of the hole.

Now with his torchlight and net at the ready, and his heart racing in his chest, he turned on his light and quickly peered over the edge.

In an instant Mr Wilf's powerful torch beam filled the cave with light, but on scanning around he was only to be disappointed once again to see there was nothing down there. Although his light beam was very bright, it couldn't reach in the little cave where he had seen the parcels, because it couldn't be seen from the position he was knelt.

So Mr Wilf returned to his barrow to get his rope, which he tied one end around a tree and the other around his waist, and once again he began to scale down the deep hole, but safely this time. On touchdown he immediately looked into the little cave where he couldn't see from above, but this time he noticed that there had been some new additions to Chase Me Chase Me's little collection.

To his surprise one of them was Nanna Norser's bust 50-inch TV, there was also a desktop printer and some more of Mr Wilf's spares and tools too.

"Hmmmm, that's an interesting development" said Mr Wilf, and pausing for a quick think he began tweaking his moustache to give him an idea of what to do next. When he got one he started gathering up all the little parcels and he began carrying them up the hole and loading them into his barrow. By the time he had got everything up and loaded it was already nearing dinner time, so he decided to make tracks as quickly as he could towards home.

Competition Time

No sooner had Mr Wilf arrived home he headed straight to his shed where he began restocking it with all the little parcels, putting them back where they were supposed to be, and after resetting his trap for Chase Me Chase Me's return he went back inside the house to make himself the most splendid dinner. This was on account of that he would be missing supper tonight while attending the competition in Leeds.

After consuming this annual pre-competition feast he then decided it was MOUSTACHE PREPARATION TIME! (Unfortunately the description of Mr Wilf's actual preparation cannot be divulged in this story, as Mr Wilf feels that it would give his competitor's the edge that could jeopardize his chances of winning any moustache competitions in the future).

Teatime soon came and Mr Wilf was fed, dressed and ready for action, it was now competition time. There he now stood looking in the mirror in his best suit topped off with a fresh carnation and admiring what he thought was his moustache at it's very finest, he had never seen it look so good, which made him more than sure that he would win again, just on its magnificence alone. Although he did have some inside knowledge he had picked up from gossip in the handlebar moustache community, that his nearest rival in the competition had just recently contracted flu, and like anyone in the moustache world knows, snot takes all the bouncy condition out of the handlebar moustache that is needed to keep it trained in position. So he was onto a dead cert he thought, and he couldn't have been much happier when he set off the catch his train.

Once at the train station he stood there on the platform so very proud, with his ticket in his hand and his moustache preened to perfection. He had the biggest smile on his face as he was so sure he would win, so sure he even began reciting a winner's speech to himself in his head all the way to Leeds on the train.

He was so distracted by compiling this speech, he was totally unaware of his surroundings and all the attention he was getting from onlookers and admirers pointing at his moustache on the train. Nor did he hear his name being called out on the address system on arrival at Leeds requesting him to go straight to the information desk. He just walked through the station as though on autopilot, practicing his speech in his head. He jumped straight into a taxi and off to the venue he went. On arrival at the hotel where the competition was being held, he was met by a group of concerned organizers and friends who eagerly greeted him, unfortunately though they were all bearing bad news.

"Mr Wilf, we've just received a message from Nana Norser, she sounded frantic over the phone, she said the grandkids have gone off to play chase me or something and wants them back in for their supper, and now she's getting a bit worried as to where they might be, Nana said that you will know what she's on about?"

Mr Wilf knew exactly what Nana was on about alright and he was devastated at the news. He couldn't believe it, the timing of something like this happening when he was so sure he would win the competition again. Despite it being a bitter pill to swallow he decided to do what any good granddad would do, he gave his apologies and said his usual cheery-bye before jumping back into the taxi he came in, and set off home as fast as his ride would take him.

All the way back he didn't speak to the driver or think about the competition once, his mind was too busy thinking about what to do when he got home. Arriving at his address he was in so much of a hurry, he didn't even waste time waiting for any change from the taxi driver, who he had obviously overpaid by at least ten pounds. He just paid up and shot into the house to get changed into his old gardening clobber as quick as he could. Then after grabbing the torch light he headed out into the garden, where after checking that the train signal on his shed was still in the empty position, he set off down the garden path through the gate and across the fields to once again enter Spooker's Wood.

This time though instead of heading straight towards the old mine workings where he thought he would probably end up, he took the path towards Nana's house firstly to pick up the kids' trail from there, just in case he was wrong.

A little time later, about a mile into his journey he found the path at the rear of Nana's house, where he noticed straight away that there were indeed little children's footprints, but they were also accompanied by big boot prints as well. To which Mr Wilf immediately began to follow, and as he predicted they were heading to the old mine workings. Only about five minutes further on his way, just about the same place where he had the run in with Cammo man, he heard his grandchildren's voices and they were laughing and giggling too. So Mr Wilf got down on his hands and knees and slowly began to crawl towards where all the excitement was coming from, and when he was close he parted the long gauze to take a peek. When he did he was absolutely flabbergasted to see that on the exact same mound of grass where he nearly sat on cammo man was all his grandchildren, and they were sat playing cards with Chase Me Chase Me, who just so happened to be wearing one of Mr Wilf's spare trilby's and smoking what looked like one of Nana's Cuban cigars as well. The source of the laughter he heard came from the excitement that was created in a Take Two card game they were all playing. It was when Chase Me Chase Me was dealt the last deuce in the deck and he had to pick up eight extra cards, and he was making funny Roboty faces to make them laugh. It made Mr Wilf laugh too, so much so he had to quickly cover his mouth with his hand.

More surprisingly and a first for Mr Wilf, was when he heard Chase Me Chase Me changing his voice each time he called each of his grandchildren by name. He changed from using his usual Robotic voice to mimicking Nana Norser, then to Mr Fabooni, and he had got his Italian accent down to a T. What made the kids laugh most of all was when he imitated Granddads voice, which was nearly spot on.

It was such a nice sight to see, so much so Mr Wilf could have watched and listened to them all night long, and he didn't want to spoil it by interrupting their fun.

The trouble was it was starting to get dark and Nana Norser would be getting really worried by now, and she might even be tempted to inform the Grimp next door and Mr Wilf certainly didn't want him getting involved.

So Mr Wilf decided to pluck up a bit of courage to make a gentle entrance by just stepping out of the bushes and saying something like, "Hiya everybody, it's Granddad here." He stood up and parted the thicket, and he was just going to step out and say exactly that, when unexpectedly a beam of light came down from the sky lighting up the entire area. It was so bright and dazzling that everyone had to put their hands up to shield their eyes, then all of a sudden this beam narrowed and seemed to just concentrate on Chase Me Chase Me alone, who then began lifting off the ground and floating up in this beam of light. When Mr Wilf looked up to see where the light came from, to his astonishment he saw it was indeed a flying saucer, just like the one Mr Snooby had described on his live TV interview.

Before Mr Wilf knew it George had grabbed Chase Me Chase Me's legs and he was trying to hold him down, but now he was being lifted up too. Seeing this Mr Wilf came running out from the bushes to their aid shouting at the top of his voice, "LET GO GEORGE," but before he could get there, Charlie, Evie and little Molly had also grabbed a hold of George's leg and now they were all being pulled up into this beam of light as well. Noticing this and still running as fast as he could, Mr Wilf took a gamble by taking advantage of an old raised tree stump to pull off the best flying leap ever to gain enough height to make a grab for Chase Me Chase Me's big rubber boot laces and hang on tight. Still it was no use, now they were all being slowly pulled up in the beam and they were all now too high for anyone to let go.

As they neared the underside of the craft the humming noise got louder and it was now clearly visible to them all that the light was coming from and opening, which they were all somehow pulled through, then a door closed behind them as they disappeared inside. The craft then made a humming noise that seemed to get louder, just like a washing machine going into its fastest spin cycle, and without warning it then just buzzed off straight up and within a blink of an eye it vanished into deep space!

The next thing Mr Wilf was aware was when he found himself sat upright in a seat, but he couldn't physically move or speak. He could move his eyes and looking out of the very corner, he could see that George, Charlie, Evie, Molly and Chase Me Chase Me were all sitting alongside him, and they were all in exactly the same condition.

They were in a small room that looked as if it was all silver metallic, even the seating too, but it smelt like the reptile house at Chester Zoo. Suddenly out of the peripheral vision of his other eye, he saw a big shadow coming down the corridor and then from around the corner appeared two big Aliens. They looked more like lizards in the face, they had tails but they walked upright and stood about 7 foot tall and were very muscular. They wore tunic-style clothing with holes in the backside where their lizard tails poked out.

Once they were in full view of everyone, one of the Aliens began to speak, but without even opening its mouth. "We don't need you humans, we only wanted the machine, but we can't take you back just now it's too dangerous, there are too many other humans watching out for us." Both the Aliens then turned to each other and began talking in their language, which sounded more like screeching, but when they had finished talking the upshot of their conversation was that they had decided to take their prisoners to their base.

One of the lizard Aliens then picked up a glass looking wand thingamajig and pointed it directly at their captives and put them under some kind of spell that made them all automatically stand up and follow the Aliens in line, and marched them down a corridor and into what looked like the command deck. Using the wand again the Alien then sat them all in front of a large window or TV screen, showing the view outside the ship, where they could now only watch helplessly as they journeyed deeper into space.

To Mr Wilf's surprise they went to the Moon! But not to the bit we can see, they went over the top and to the dark side.

On landing they saw hundreds of spaceships just like the one they were in, all lined up next to large buildings that were well lit. When the spacecraft's doors opened it sounded very busy with activity outside and Mr Wilf was more than curious to know what it was all about. He was about to find out, when all of a sudden the two Aliens pointed the wand thing at them again, making them all stand up and turn to face the door in single file. Chase Me Chase Me was at the front, the kids were in the middle and Mr Wilf was at the back. They were all then marched off in line towards the door with the two Aliens walking in front. One of the Aliens was walking backwards still pointing this glass-looking wand at them. As they neared the ramp to descend towards the ground next to what looked like a huge aircraft hangar, Chase Me Chase Me suddenly seemed to snap out of his hypnotic trance and he quickly leapt forward and snatched the wand from the Alien's claws, at the same time hand palming it straight in it's mush, sending the Alien somersaulting head over tail down the ramp.

Even before the other Alien had chance to react, Chase Me Chase Me kicked it straight up the backside and he kicked it so hard that its tail nearly went up its bum, making it scream out loud just like a big girl, before it went falling down the ramp landing face first into the lunar dirt.

Then for some unknown reason Chase Me Chase Me knew how to close the spacecraft doors and use the wand control stick, which he then used to sit his friends down in the command deck, where once again he knew how to start the engine, which fired up instantly, and began to make that whirring washing machine spin cycle sound, and before everyone knew it, they were up and off and back into space.

Within just a few minutes the craft had already landed again and no sooner it had, the door suddenly opened... And you'll never guess where this time?... They had only landed in Nana Norser's back garden! Chase Me Chase Me then opened the doors, and using the wand control stick the same way the Alien's had used it, he pointed it at the kids and marched them down the ramp, but for some reason leaving Mr Wilf still onboard. Who could now only listen as he heard Chase Me Chase Me bid each of them a cheery-bye in his Robot voice, and by the sound of it Nana was there too, because he could hear the kids telling her they had been in space.

Chase Me Chase Me then came back inside and shut the spaceship's door behind him, no sooner he had the engines made the full spin cycle sound, up and off in the air they went.

Within only a few moments the spaceship had landed once again, but this time and to Mr Wilf's surprise they had landed on the rooftop car park of the hotel where the annual handlebar moustache competition was in Leeds.

Not only that, he could even see the town hall clock on the big screen inside the spaceship, he was still in time for the senior judging.

Then using the wand control stick again, Chase Me Chase Me marched Mr Wilf down the spaceship ramp, over the empty rooftop car park and straight towards the service elevator where he boarded him on the lift, he then pressed the ground floor button and when the lift voice announced to clear the doors, only then did Chase Me Chase Me take the spell off Mr Wilf with the Alien wand.

Before Mr Wilf could even react or utter a single word to Chase Me Chase Me, the lift door had shut in his face and he was already descending down to the hotel reception level. Even before he could come out of his daze or gather his wits, the elevator voice had announced "ground floor" and the door then suddenly whooshed open to reveal a packed hotel foyer where he was instantly mobbed by all his fans, friends and event organizers who were all really happy to see him.

"We were hoping you were coming back, but

you're cutting it a bit fine though hey" "You had us all worried" they all similarly said but still very glad to see him all the same.

Before Mr Wilf knew it he was being patted on the back and herded into the awaiting packed ballroom, and again before he knew it, he was already standing on the stage with the rest of the seniors in front of hundreds of people ready to be judged!

Despite Mr Wilf's traumatic space experience and his less than perfect dress sense for the occasion, he won the competition outright! He was made the overall winner. Not only that, because he had already won it five times he also picked up the trophy for good and he was also given the honorary title of Grand Tashmaster to boot. This meant that now he automatically qualified to be a judge as well.

The problem was, when Mr Wilf was prompted to make his acceptance speech, the one he had rehearsed on the train earlier, which he was hoping to make everyone laugh with as he usually did, his mind was blank and he just stood there in a silent daze with a big grin on his face instead. To which everyone must have assumed was down to Mr Wilf being overwhelmed by the honour bestowed upon him and the whole occasion.

The local press however were more interested in meeting the deadline for the morning papers rather than the sentiment. They kept trying to get him to respond to the question, "what were his feelings at that very moment" they asked him over and over again, until finally he answered, but when he did he could only repeat the same phrase to every question they posed. "Over the moon, over the moon, over the moon".

Although the press were totally bemused by this, the audience must have thought it made him sound more endearing and clapped every time he said it. And before Mr Wilf could be asked anymore questions, he was whisked off in the nick of time by his mates into the bar to celebrate. It was traditional for the winner to make the obligatory first toast by drinking a trophy cup full of brandy and by the time he had finished this ritual, if Mr Wilf had a tale to tell anyone there, he was now too incapable of telling it.

When the celebrations finally came to an end and it was time for everyone to go home, Mr Wilf was put in the winner's limousine and sent on his merry way. While in the limo though, and seeing as he had never experienced this sort of luxury before he couldn't help but take advantage of the free hospitality bar, so by the time he arrived home he'd had far too much to drink and he was a lot more than being a little tipsy.

After bidding the white knight in shining armor (the chauffeur) a loud cheery-bye, loud enough to wake half the close, he tottered off down his garden path and straight around to the back door which had the bigger key and was easier to open on these sort of occasions.

On arriving at his back door he automatically began rumaging for his keys, the while he was doing so he just happened to take a glance towards his shed when the security light came on and he noticed that the train signal was in the up position.

But still being very tipsy, Mr Wilf couldn't believe his eyes at first and he had to refocus a few times to make sure they weren't playing tricks on him. Realizing the signal was indeed up, he put his finger to his lips and made the "shhhhh" sound to himself before walking very quietly and zigzagigly towards his shed. Eventually finding the window he pressed his face straight up against the glass and peered into the darkness inside.

"I knowz your in there somewhere ya little rascal," he slurred. "I can seeeee youuuuu... I want... I want... a word... hiccup, hiccup... with you, my little Robotiwots. Come on... give ya old man a big kiss, hmmm... awww come on, I know you're in there Chase Me Chase Me." he said.

All of a sudden to Mr Wilf's delight, he saw a dark figure on the other side of the glass that looked as if it was standing upright and coming closer towards the window and right up to the bars of the cage trap inside. Seeing this figure standing there Mr Wilf hurriedly shuffled around towards the shed door as quick as he could, but just as he was going to pull the lever that released the mechanism that opened the door, Mr Wilf suddenly hesitated and paused to have a think for a moment... hmmm? And after doing so he made a precondition to the occupant inside.

"Hic, hic... now listen to me here Chase Me Chase Me, if I let you out ..hiccup hiccup.. you've gotta promise me they'll be no more flying about in spasheshwips and kicking Aliens and people up the arse, and no running around in the woods scaring... hic... hic... people... hiccup... either," adding, "And if you do you can come inside and have a nice cup of tea with me... hiccup... and we'll have a nice little chat if ya like." Mr Wilf paused for a moment waiting for an answer before releasing the catch. Then he got one, when he heard a loud deep voice from inside the shed reply, "I PROMISE THEN." So with this acceptable answer and without thinking anymore about it, Mr Wilf went to pull the lever that opened the door. However, as he did he realized something wasn't quite right and different about Chase Me Chase Me's voice, and he couldn't help make the remark,

"That is so very funny, it's remarkable how good you can mimic voices, I must say you do a marvelous impression of Sgt Grimper, hiccup...

tell me how is it you can do that."

Before he could say another word the shed door suddenly sprang wide open and standing there in its place was a big dark figure, who on stepping out into the light and to Mr Wilf's absolute horror then said,

"Because it is Sgt Grimper."

Mr Wilf could have died right there on the spot, his jaw nearly dropped down to his knees, making that urrrrr noise (just like the one you make when you're not only disappointed but surprised too) at the very sobering sight of the real Sgt Grimper stood there looking at him. Then Mr Wilf noticed something different about Sgt Grimper, he was grinning from ear to ear and he had a really friendly look on his face, especially when he went on to say,

"I would love to come inside your home and have that cup of tea and that nice little chat if you dont mind." Then gesturing with his hand he courteously invited Mr Wilf towards the house door, "after you Mr Wilf" he said. He was very jolly about it too, which was a big surprise to Mr Wilf, who was by now beginning to think he was being humoured by the Grimp, just like he had humoured old Mr Snooby and he had now probably relegated him to the same level as Snubber's, especially after hearing what he had just said outside the garden shed.

Then he noticed something else that was unusual about the Grimp, he was now covered in the White Goo stuff, which he must have got on him while sat in the damp area of the shed, because he was now glowing in the dark.

On entering the house the Grimp was ever so kind, opening the door for Mr Wilf, he even insisted on making the tea for them both and was ever so complementary to Mr Wilf on his competition victory and his trophies.

It wasn't long before they both found themselves sat by the fireside slurping tea and dunking biscuits, and it was then Mr Wilf took advantage of the situation, while the Grimp was under the influence of the Goo and he was still under the influence of booze, space lag and the Alien control stick, he was quite happy to tell Grimp the truth, the whole truth and nothing but the truth, just like a confession and get everything off his chest, telling him his entire story up to that point. But when he started to tell his story, the Grimp who was still wearing a big smile on his face interrupted him and said,

"There... there Mr Wilf, don't you worry, I know everything, I don't know why but I just do, I saw it all in my head when I was sat in your shed. I can't explain how, but for some reason, I now have a message for you as well, and it's something very, very important."

Hearing this astonishing statement Mr Wilf sat upright in his seat eager to learn more about what this message was. His face was now transfixed on the Grimp's face, ready to hang on to his every word in anticipation of what it might be. Surprisingly then, Sgt Grimper suddenly stood up from his chair and said, "But I better leave it until tomorrow it's far too important to tell you in your condition considering all you have been through you might forget it by the morning and I can see you need your rest."

All the while Mr Wilf was saying, "but... but..." wanting Sgt Grimper to tell him more.

"It's no use saying but... but... Mr Wilf, I've had a hard day and I'm in need of a shower and bed too."

Before Mr Wilf knew it Sgt Grimper had bid a hasty goodbye and had left by the back door and was already heading down the garden path towards his home.

Mr Wilf was also very tired, so he was quite content to just leave it until tomorrow. He needed his bed so badly that he even skipped his pipe and didn't bother with his milk, he just decided to go to bed and no sooner his head hit the pillow he was in the world's deeeeepest of sleeps, and there he stayed with the happiest grin on his face, snoring till morning.

The Next Day

It was another bright and sunny start to the day in the small town of Normantofts, but not for Mr Wilf, for this particular Wednesday morning instead of being up and about bright and early and making himself busy as usual, he was still fast asleep snoring his head off in bed!

He was so tired he could have slept the clock round, but like on all those occasions when you're having a really nice deep spleep (a spleep is a sleep after consuming alcoholic beverages) the phone rang.

"Derring... derring... derring." it went, but it went on and on.

Until its annoying persistence eventually paid off, finally making Mr Wilf begin to stir. Still being mostly asleep he reached out of his duvet and made a fumbling grab for the phone and quickly pulled it under his quilt to answer.

"Cough... cough... splutter... Hewo, errrr, errrr, Hello who this is... I mean... cough... cough... splutter... splutter, who is it" he asked, but typically there was no answer at the other end, just the sound of disengaged tone.

Being too tired to even care, Mr Wilf just put the phone down and nestled back deeper into his duvet to continue on with his nap. But it wasn't any use now he had been disturbed he just couldn't get back off to sleep, so he decided he might as well get up.

After a massive stretch followed by a mega yawn, Mr Wilf summoned up the right amount of energy to make the leap of no return out of bed, however when he did he unexpectedly let out the loudest of farts which was so powerful it virtually propelled him straight to his feet without any effort at all.

"Oh dear I don't like the sound of that," he muttered, but at the same time it also gave Mr Wilf an inclination to what he had been up to the night before, and considering how rough he felt as well and putting two and two together, he figured he must have been out celebrating! But celebrating what he thought, his mind was completely blank, the details from the night before were a total mystery to him and things were about to become even more confusing when he proceeded to get dressed. On reaching for his clothes that he usually put on the bedside chair after he had got undressed, he couldn't find them, they weren't there? That is until he noticed himself in the dressing table mirror and realized why, because he still had them on! But what threw a new spanner in the works of his already clouded mind, was not only was he fully dressed, which he could sort of understand especially after a night out celebrating, but what he couldn't figure out was why was he wearing his old gardening clobber.

"Hmmmmmmm... this is so very strange" he muttered to himself, and he began vigorously scratching his head trying to think how that could be? At first nothing came to mind, but then on shuffling into the bathroom to brush his teeth and scrape off the Berber carpet that beer fairies put on men's tongues, he suddenly began to have flashbacks from the night before which didn't make sense at first, that is until he looked at his face in the mirror. It was on noticing how sad his moustache looked this morning after all the preparation it had received, that jogged his memory, he suddenly remembered winning the competition, so he hurried downstairs as quick as he could and went straight into the kitchen. Lo and behold, there above the fireplace were all his winning trophies neatly positioned in a row, just as he remembered, but the clothes were still a mystery though.

None the less it didn't stop him going about his morning routine of making his breakfast as usual, just happy in the knowledge he had actually won the competition, and as far as he was concerned that's all that mattered to him.

A few moments later, just as Mr Wilf was scooping up the last remnants of milk from his cereal bowl, he happened to take a glance through the window to check the weather outside, but when he did he noticed that something was different and out of place. Still being in a bit of a daze it took him quite a few seconds until he realized what it was.

The shed door shut tight and the train signal was up in the air! Which could only mean one thing: his trap was full! He dropped his spoon in his dish, jumped straight to his feet and shot outside to the shed as quick as he could. Without considering who could be in there other than Chase Me Chase Me, he wasted no time in pulling the lever that released the door, but when the door came springing wide open to reveal the captive inside... instead of his invention stood there with outstretched arms to greet him, it was the last person he wanted to see. To his absolute horror, you will never guess who it was? It was only Mr Golding the milkman, who was now standing there glowing red in the face with steam practically coming out of his ears.

He immediately began to shout his protest, "WELL IT'S ABOUT TIME I MUST SAY! I'VE RUN MY MOBILE FLAT RINGING YOU, AN HOUR I'VE BEEN STUCK IN HERE, I'M LATE ON MY ROUND NOW, IT'S A WONDER MY MILK HASN'T GONE SOUR, I WISH I HAD RUNG THE POLICE FIRST," he blasted angrily.

"But-but but-but," stammered Mr Wilf, struggling to gather his words so he could explain, but it was no good, Mr Golding was having none of it! He pushed Mr Wilf to one side and set off out of the garden yelling,

"YOU'RE FOR IT NOW, JUST WAIT UNTIL SGT GRIMPER HEARS ABOUT THIS ONE, HE SAID IT WAS A MISUNDERSTANDING THE LAST TIME... WELL WE WILL SEE ABOUT THAT!"

Before Mr Wilf could respond to that, Goldy was already out of the gate and had gone marching down the street! Once again this left Mr Wilf stood there scratching his head, but this time trying to figure out why on Earth Goldy would be looking in his shed in the first place.

"Oh dear, oh dear, it looks like I'm for it now," he mumbled, and because there was nothing he could do to amend the situation, he just shrugged his shoulders and went back indoors regardless. But as he was stepping over the threshold of his door, Goldy's words about informing Sgt Grimper were still ringing in his ears, which jogged his memory and reminded him of the Grimp actually letting him in the house the night before and making the tea for them both, even bits about having a conversation with him about winning the competition, but he still couldn't understand why the Grimp was at his house in the first place.

In order to find this out Mr Wilf decided to give

the old moustache a chance. He lit up his pipe and sat in his rocker tweaking his moustache while puffing away and making smoke rings trying to remember what he could.

Which wasn't much at first, but tracing back from when he went to bed he got the mental picture of Sgt Grimper saying he had something important to tell him in the morning and it was too important to tell him in his condition last night. He could remember that because it was the very last thing the Grimp had said to him! So without hesitation Mr Wilf jumped up from his rocking chair and got straight on the phone to the Grimp to ask him what this important message was. But after ringing him and not receiving an answer straight away he came to the conclusion that the Grimp was probably still in bed, and not wanting to disturb him he quickly put down the phone.

None the less he was still very keen to hear what this important message was and impatient to find that out he decided to pay the Grimp a visit instead. On reckoning that by the time he got down to his house the Grimp would be up and about, if not he might get some answers from someone else who lived down there too.

Mr Wilf hurriedly put on his hat and coat and set off as quick as he could out of the back door and went straight down the garden path across the fields and back into Spooker's wood. He took the direct path that led straight towards the Grimp's house, and all the while he was marching he couldn't help thinking about this important message and what it could be. It also occurred to him that this memory might not actually be real and it all could have been just a figment of his imagination, because although some parts of yesterday's events were definitely coming back to him slowly but surely, overall everything was still a bit hazy and some still didn't make much sense at all. The more he thought about it the more desperate he was to get a reality check from someone else, just to satisfy himself he wasn't losing his mind.

On arriving at Nana Norser's, Mr Wilf firstly went next door to call in on the Grimp, which was his main intention, but all the curtains were drawn in his house. Realizing he might actually be still in bed because he had been on nights, Mr Wilf went to see Nana who he also intended to visit anyway.

"Ayup Nana", he shouted whilst bobbing his head around the door

"Is that you Mr Wilfers?" responded Nana, who immediately came whirring out the living room on her mobility scooter to greet him. "Here... here..." she said.

"Come in and look at mi new Telly," she insisted

excitedly, pulling at his arm and practically turning her scooter on the spot to lead Mr Wilf back into the living room to proudly show off her new TV.

"What you reckon to that then?" Nana said with a big grin on her face and staring up in admiration of her brand new toy. To Mr Wilf's amazement, there in the room was what looked like a giant cinema screen to him, as he only had a modest TV set at home. It was a brand new 100-inch smart TV.

"My, my, couldn't you get one bigger?" Wilfers sarcastically replied, and before he could say another word Nana had wasted no time in turning it on and was already demonstrating all of its functions and capabilities. No matter how interesting this display was though, Mr Wilf had more pressing things on his mind and he was in a hurry to find out if Nana could help piece together what had actually happened to him the day before.

"Nana, do you remember yesterday at all?" he asked hopefully trying to get her attention away from her new pride and joy.

"Yes, yes of course I do, did ya win again Wilfers?" Nana replied, with her eyes still fixed on the Telly and concentrating more on flicking around its channels with the remote.

"Yes indeed I did, I did indeed," Wilfers proudly exclaimed.

"Ha haaa! I knew it, no one can beat my Wilfers

Whiskers", replied Nana, still more focused on the TV. However before Mr Wilf could continue with his urgent enquiry, Nana had accidentally landed on the local TV news channel which just happened to be reporting on more strange lights in the area, with sightings of spacecraft seen hovering over an industrial estate where several nearby wholesale premises had been broken into in the night and large amounts of equipment stolen.

This got Mr Wilf's and Nana's undivided attention straight away. Both were now watching intently as the TV item then featured an eyewitness from the adjacent borough who was describing a craft he saw hovering over a warehouse. It just happened to fit the same description of the craft Mr Wilf and the kids had been on a ride in the night before.

Finally the TV presenter rounded off the news item leaving the viewers with the question "Who or what it could be?" No sooner she did, both Wilfers and Nana couldn't help shouting out the answer to the TV, "IT'S CHASE ME CHASE ME!" Suddenly realizing they had come to the same conclusion, they burst into laughter at the same time, but as the laughter subsided to mere chuckles, it was only then that Nana decided to drop the bombshell that she did.

"It fetched the kids home in one just like that last night, worried me sick it did, I was trying to phone you Wilfers!", she said.

"No, no," interrupted Wilfers. "I remember now I was there too."

"No you wasn't," insisted Nana.

"Yes I was Nana," Wilfers equally insisted. "I was in the spaceship too, it took me to the competition in Leeds and that's how I got there and won!"

Nana's face strained for a short moment, squinting her eyes to think, and then replied, "Well the kids never said anything about being with you last night."

Hearing this Mr Wilf just shrugged his shoulders and went into the kitchen and shouted, "Cup of tea Nana?"

He hadn't given up on her yet, as he knew through his past experience with Nana that a tea break was essential because if he pressed her too much on anything too taxing she would just go to sleep... or at least pretend to.

Nana Norser was a Nana to many children and on lots of occasions she looked after her grandchildren's, children's children, for school drop-offs or while their parents were working late or just having a break from the little rascals, which she was always overjoyed to do so. She just loved the company and was still quite capable of caring for them too, and because it was another school run day and it wouldn't be long before those little rascals all came crashing in.

Reality Change

Wilfers and Nana were soon sat by the giant TV having a nice cup of tea and biscuits, so Mr Wilf decided to have another go at Nana to see exactly what she knew.

"Nana, do you remember last night?"

"Last night?" Nana repeated as she sat squinting her eyes tighter to listen.

"Well Nana?" insisted Mr Wilf.

"Yes... yes... of course I do, that Chase Me Chase Me had the kids playing out again and it didn't fetch them back till late, I nearly asked the Grimp to go find em for me, worried me sick it did," Nana added.

"Well do you know where that Robot comes from Nana?" enquired Wilfers

"Well..." she said, pausing a moment to squint... Then to his surprise she replied, "The kids said you made him Wilfers and he lives in your shed" But she said this with a confused look on her face, as though waiting for him to acknowledge that it was indeed true.

Even so, still insistent on getting the answers he required Mr Wilf pressed Nana further.

"What about the spaceship Nana, I didn't make that" he said with a big smile. By now Nana was getting confused and a little tired, and all she could be bothered to come up with was, "It'll be one of Mr Snooby's spaceships then!" She said yawningly and hinting for a little nap. Realizing he had probably pushed her too far, Mr Wilf gathered up the cups and plates and took them into the kitchen, leaving Nana to have her overdue mid morning nap.

Fortunately, while Mr Wilf was rinsing off the dishes in the sink he spotted Sgt Grimper's bald head over the other side of the fence, so he went straight outside to confront him. He was walking up and down the garden mowing his lawn, he was wearing a string vest and his braces were hanging down and it looked like he had just got out of bed.

"MR GRIMPER, MR GRIMPER," Mr Wilf shouted over the fence and the noise of the lawnmower, managing to get his attention. The Grimp switched off his mower and came over to meet him at the fence.

"Ho, hi there Mr Wilf," the Grimp said. "Is everything ok?" he enquired, but he was unusually smiling for a change...

"Yes fine Mr Grimper," replied Mr Wilf, "I was just wondering if there was something you wanted to tell me this morning?" he enquired hopefully, taking the Grimp's grinning smile as an indication he did indeed have something to tell him. Surprisingly the Grimp's face then screwed up straining to understand what Mr Wilf was talking about and now looking more than puzzled he replied, "Something to tell you."

"Yes at my house last night you came to see me remember" said Mr Wilf, who was now starting to show his frustration as the Grimp's face began to strain even more, which wasn't making Mr Wilf confident in what he thought he could remember himself.

Then Sgt Grimper suddenly remembered something, "Oh yes that's right I do have a message to give you, I got it from from the wife, it's here in my notepad, she wrote it in this morning, it didn't make sense until you just mentioned it," said the Grimp.

"A message from your wife" Mr Wilf repeated in astonishment, as the Grimp went on to say.

"Yes that's right I remember now, I came to your house to ask you to stop scaring Mr Golding... that's right, but as I recall it was all a big mistake and we sorted all that out... didn't we?" The Grimp paused to scratch his chin before continuing. "Which leads me on to my wife's message this morning, it says that Mr Golding went and got himself locked in your shed or something, now was that it?" said the Grimp with the big happy smile returning to his face, only to see Mr Wilf looking back at him, absolutely baffled.

"Is that it, there's nothing else you want to tell me, are you sure Mr Grimper"

"Oh err... err... no... yes... oh, wait a minute there is a bit more here," replied the Grimp

"Yes, yes" Mr Wilf said excitedly, hoping it was something more important, only to hear the Grimp go on to say, "Ah yes, the last bit of the message on my pad is... you'll be needing a new milkman, Mr Golding said he's too scared to deliver you any more milk!"

"And that's all... there's nothing else," replied Mr Wilf disappointedly.

"I'm afraid that's all I can tell you Mr Wilf sorry," said the Grimp on returning back to his task of mowing his lawn.

As he did Mr Wilf noticed there was something very strange about the Grimp, he didn't seem to be his normal self, he usually wanted to get to the bottom of things, but now he was behaving as though he was indifferent and without a care in the world. He also kept that same big smile on his face too, which was definitely out of character for the Grimp. Mr Wilf called him over again to check.

"Excuse me, Mr Grimper, Mr Grimper?"
The Grimp once again turned off his mower and came over to the fence and still wearing a big grin on his face.

"I was wondering... if you do remember anything else, especially about last night, you will let me know won't you"

"Oh yes, of course I will," said the Grimp, "But I

can't think what it is you're after Mr Wilf, I definitely can't but I will certainly keep it in mind and if I do remember something I will let you know."

Still convinced that the Grimp had changed somehow, Mr Wilf felt compelled to enquire about his wellbeing. "Are you sure you're ok Mr Grimper?" he asked, but he wasn't quite expecting the answer he was about to hear.

"Oh, I've never felt better in my life Mr Wilf, I've woken up today like a new man, I feel fantastic and from today I'm going to start as I mean to go on," he said.

"How's that then?" enquired a now very surprised Mr Wilf, only to hear the Grimp go on to say, "Well, I've been thinking about all this police work, locking people up and dealing with crime, it doesn't make sense to me anymore, we should be much nicer to people and try to help the less fortunate, those at the bottom of the ladder" adding "It all seems so very wrong to me and I'm going to do something about it." On that note he returned to his mower and started mowing the garden again, with the same big smile on his face without a care in the world.

Mr Wilf couldn't believe his ears, he was totally bewildered at this new changed attitude of the Grimp, he just didn't know what to make of it, but whatever was causing this change needed some special consideration. So he immediately went back inside Nana's house, where after making himself a nice cup of tea he sat at the kitchen table to have a ponder by his usual way of tweaking his moustache, trying to work out why the Grimp had no memory of the night before and why he was in such an unusually good mood today.

The first thing that came into his mind was the White Goo, because he remembered how it affected him when he got some on his hands in the garden and how it had sent him funny. It was only a little smear and only on his hands a few seconds, whereas the Grimp was covered in it last night and it must have been on him for ages before he had the opportunity to scrub it off, so it could have permanently affected him, he sumised?

Well that was one theory he had and the only one he had at the moment. Mr Wilf still wasn't that sure about anything at this point and his only option now was to wait until the grandchildren arrived from school to see if they could fill in the rest of the blanks for him. Because up until now if it hadn't been for Nana's input, he was sure he would have lost his marbles and gone completely round the bend, so it would definitely be worth waiting around to hear what the kids had to say he thought.

After reaching that conclusion Mr Wilf went back into the living room where Nana was already snoozing away, and where he also got himself comfortable on the settee and within only a few moments he was snoozing too, both now snoring in unison like a pair of old Moose in deep sleep.

As the pair lay there the clock turned round and the minutes soon became an hour and more. The next thing Mr Wilf knew, was when all the grandkids came crashing into the living room and on seeing their granddad laying there, they couldn't resist jumping up and down on him to wake him up "GRANDDAD, GRANDDAD, WAKE UP," leaving him no other choice but to get up or be trampled to death by his crazy little Grandkids.

"Oh I've been waiting for you," said Granddad yawningly, and being so very eager to see them he had one big stretch, and being careful not to trump this time he jumped straight to his feet. However, just as he was going to gather all his grandchildren together to start questioning them about what they could tell him about the night before, Charlie handed his Granddad an envelope and it was addressed to his parents. As he did his brother George took it upon himself to speak up for him

"Our Charlie has been told off at school by the teacher for making up stories, and getting angry with the other boys when they laughed at him and now everyone in school is laughing at the both of us now Granddad."

"What stories?" enquired Granddad with a look

of concern on his face.

"About us going for a ride in a spaceship and Chase Me Chase Me kicking that man in a lizard suit up the bum." Charlie blurted defiantly.

Hearing this great news Granddad punched the air in excitement," Yes I knew it, I knew it" he said. It was like music to his ears, it was just such a relief to hear it wasn't a figment of his imagination and he wasn't losing his mind after all. Although that being the case, the trouble was now, not only did he have to come to terms with the fact that they all had actually been taken to the moon by Aliens, but also a Robot he had invented was still on the loose, flying around in one of their spaceships and by all accounts according to the news on TV, he was nicking stuff too!

"So it all really, really happened," Granddad said, staring up at the ceiling with a look of wonderment all over his face. Just at that moment Nana came speeding into the room, interrupting as usual.

"HERE, HERE," she shouted to the kids. "When Chase Me Chase Me dropped you off in that thingamajig last night where was your granddad then?" she demanded squintingly. To which George, Charlie, Evie and Mollie all equally blurted out the same reply, "In the spaceship, Nana... derrrrr."

"There I told you Nana," said Wilfers with a big

grin on his face, happy he was right, but almost instantaneously realizing it was another bitter sweet moment, because he had not only proved all his memories were true, but now he also had to contend with the fact that he had seen lots of Aliens on the moon who were preparing something sinister as well, and that he thought could be exactly what old Mr Snooby had been talking about outside the town hall the other day! They were preparing to INVADE THE PLANET EARTH!

So what will it mean for everyone if they do? What he found the most puzzling was what did his invention Chase Me Chase Me have to do with all of this, why were the Aliens so keen to get their claws on him? But now perhaps he might have a chance to finally find that out.

"Right then" Granddad Wilf announced getting everyone's attention, "Gather round everybody, we're all going to have a nice little questions and answers game."

On hearing this the kids excitedly gathered in a huddle around their Granddad Wilf's feet where he had taken command of the big armchair by the old stone fireplace. When Nana had finally nudged her scooter in closer so she could participate, they all sat quietly waiting for the game to start.

When everybody was ready Mr Wilf began.

"Right, this one is for the kids only Nana! Right kids, when did you all first meet Chase Me Chase Me" he asked, to which Charlie instantly blurted out, "In your shed, Granddad."

"Ha haaa," said Granddad, relieved he was actually getting somewhere.

"Was it when he put you up that tree?" he then asked. "Yes," replied Charlie.
It was this point his brother George, not wanting to be left out, spoke up.

"Yeah, but I saw him as well another time when he was at the back of Nana's house paddling in the beck and when our Charlie shouted to him he came over to us and he wanted to play."

Grandad was ecstatic at this news, he couldn't believe that he might actually be getting to the bottom of what was going on, he was so excited, he began scratching his head vigorously trying to summon up his next question... And when he had found one he said.

"But did he say where he came from?"
To which all his grandchildren blurted in unison, "In your shed" This reply made Mr Wilf sigh in frustration, he was hoping for a different answer to that. So this time he posed the question differently.

"Who taught him to do all those things he can do?"
Only again to hear them all shout out at once, "You Granddad, you did, you built him."

Mr Wilf sighed again, then posed a different

question, but now he insisted they answer one at a time and only put their hands up if they knew the answer.

"Did he say why I built him then?" he asked.

Now everyone's hands were up in the air at this question, even Nana's!

"Go on then Charlie, seeing as you were the first to meet him you can go first" said Granddad.

Charlie stood to his feet and in a matter of fact voice he proudly said

"Chase Me Chase Me told me it was to teach some naughty boys a lesson, and when he had done that he had a bigger job to do and until then he had to hide in the woods."

With this new information Mr Wilf paused for a few seconds to gather his thoughts, because the second part of what Charlie had just said made no sense to him at all, which made Mr Wilf more determined to find out what was going on. To do that he had to press his grandchildren a little further, well to be truthful he wanted to squeeze every last drop of information out of them as he could before they went home.

Now he preceded very cautiously, trying find out what else they might know, because up until now it was like pulling teeth he thought.

"And did he tell you what this job was?" asked Granddad.

Again on this question everyone's hands were up

in the air and seeing as George and Charlie both had their turn, he picked Evie next. She was normally a quiet shy little girl, but now she seemed bursting at the seams to tell him something. Although little Molly had her hand up in the air she was too young to understand what was going on, and was just copying what everyone else was doing.

"Go on, Evie your turn now," said Granddad.

"Chase Me Chase Me told me that his job is to do good and stop bad things happening in the world, Grandad!"

On hearing this Granddad's face strained trying to understand what that meant, until George took it on himself to further explain his understanding of the situation on Evie's behalf.

"When there's too much badness in the world, sometimes goodness has to step in and balance things up, well that's what Chase Me Chase Me told us Granddad" said George. While wrinkling his nose, obviously showing that he didn't fully understand what that meant either.

Granddad Wilf slumped back in his chair practically overwhelmed by all this new information, so he began tweaking his moustache trying to find the right question, and when he did he leant forward and said,

"Did he say why he had to hide or why he kept running away from me."

Unfortunately this time there were no hands

up at all, instead he faced a wall of blank faces staring back at him.

"Do you know anything else? Did Chase Me Chase Me say anymore?" Granddad desperately pleaded, only to hear Charlie's disappointing reply, "No Granddad we just played out with him that's all, he didn't tell us anything else."

Then all of a sudden Nana put her hand up in the air and she looked really excited to tell what it was she knew.

"Yes Nana?" said Wilfers.

"I know... I know, he told me something" she proudly announced, but instead of giving her information straight up she decided to tease the kids with it for a bit as Nanas do. She sealed her lips, folded her arms and turned her face to one side instead. She wasn't going to relinquish her secret unless it was coaxed out from her by her grandkids pleading with her, which she knew they would. They immediately began shouting, "Tell us Nana. Go on... tell us Nana" they said while pulling at her arm. When she had heard enough begging, especially from Wilfers, only then did she decide to spill the beans, but it actually turned out to be more like a can of worms.

"Well, he told me that he's got to guard something and it's in your shed Wilfers."

At this new piece of information everyone's face was a picture, they were all sat opened-mouthed staring at Nana. In reality her face was just a focal point, everyone was in deep thought concentrating and thinking hard about what could possibly be in Granddad's shed that would need guarding.

Nana was squinting harder than ever, and Granddad Wilf was tweaking his moustache like mad... Then all of a sudden he had a eureka moment and he couldn't help just blurting the answer out, making everyone jump and nearly giving poor Nana a heart attack in the process.

"IT'S THE WHITE GOO" he yelled, then realizing his over excitement, he lowered his voice to calmly repeat it again "It's got to be the Goo," only to see that everyone else was still wearing puzzled faces, which wasn't surprising considering that he was the only one in the room who knew about the Goo, so of course it didn't make any sense to Nana or the kids.

At least it made sense to him and already Mr Wilf's mind was beginning to put two and two together and although it still only made three in his understanding of things, he now felt he was getting closer to the truth, and before he could elaborate anymore about the Goo to the rest, Nana broke all concentration again when she suddenly remembered something else.

"Hey I know, we could ask Chase Me Chase Me what's in your shed, he promised me he was coming back tomorrow."

Granddad Wilf and the kids couldn't believe their ears, but they quickly surrounded their Nana wanting to know more.

"Why is he coming back here tomorrow Nana?" they all demanded, and to everyone's amazement she replied,

"To crop mi conifers of course, he said mi conifers are blocking out the sun that gives me the vitamin D which I need to keep me healthy... well that's what Chase Me Chase Me told me anyway" said Nana.

On hearing this late contribution they all stared at their Nana with the same look of frustration written across their faces, even little Molly shook her head.

"Are you quite sure there's nothing else you might want to tell us while you're at it Nana" Wilfers sarcastically snapped, even though he was still hopeful there might be. So everyone remained silent and waited while she squinted to have another think.

Unfortunately before Nana could come out with anymore revelations it became too late when everyone suddenly heard the front door open to shouts of "We're here" from the mums and dads who had arrived to pick their kids up, and making Nana lose all concentration.

Just as the parents entered the living room Mr Wilf noticed that Charlie's letter from school was on the coffee table, and with a bit of quick thinking he snatched it up and put it in his pocket out of sight, and whispering out the corner of his mouth to little Charlie and the kids, "Leave it to me, I will deal with this later," followed by the old mum's the word gesture to the lips, and the obligatory nod with a wink (the universal code that everyone understood, even little Molly).

Luckily for Mr Wilf everyone was in such a hurry to get home for their teas and it made their visit a short one. As soon as the kids gathered up their things, everyone including Granddad who was offered a lift was ready to go and after they said their goodbye's to Nana they climbed into the family cars and set off home.

No sooner had Mr Wilf got through the front door he headed straight into the kitchen to find his faithful old rocking chair where he wasted no time in getting comfortable and sparking up his pipe. There he sat blowing smoke rings and tweaking his moustache, pondering his next move, he wasn't long in the pondering though when he suddenly got an idea of what he should do.

He jumped to his feet and went straight outside into his garden shed where he picked up his spy glass from its place, then after getting down on all fours he began investigating the White Goo substance. Firstly he needed to find out where it came from and its source. Was it coming from the old overflowing bottle garden downwardly or was it coming from the decaying power cell boxes and going upwards he wondered?

The first thing he noticed was that the White Goo glistened like miniature glitter and it resembled something that looked like a giant slug trail and it was luminous even though it wasn't dark outside yet.

This glowing trail of Goo went upwards from the boxes on the bottom shelves where the power cells were kept, and it led right up the wall and then down into the stem of the bottle garden... or you could say the other way around?

Mr Wilf then proceeded to collect some of the Goo in an empty jar using a thin blade paper scraper. All the while he was very careful not to get any on himself, reminded not only of the effect it had on him when he picked up the battery in the garden, but more so of the Grimps experience, because he didn't want to end up like him and forget everything and return back to being none the wiser again.

Although he did remember having feelings of well being and all knowing when the Goo was on his hands, but afterwards he couldn't remember what the all knowing was, and if he couldn't remember anything the next day what was the use of that he thought?

By the time Mr Wilf had gathered enough of

the Goo he had filled a whole large-sized pickle jar and after securing the lid he placed it out of harm's way, then rolled up his sleeves ready to do his next piece of handiwork and that was to fortify his shed!

This time it wasn't to keep someone or something trapped inside, but to keep whoever or whatever out! It was Nana's words that were still ringing in his ears, "It told me it had to guard something in your shed", and after he had already concluded that there was more to this Goo than meets the eye and seeing as there was nothing else of value in there, it had to be the Goo that needed protecting.

So after an immense amount of effort and working late into the night, Mr Wilf's old shed which he had once turned into a trap had now become an impenetrable fortress to keep whoever out instead! But that was the question he kept asking himself all the time he was building it... who was the Goo supposed to be kept guarded from? Was it the Aliens, he thought?

Eventually when he was sure he had fortified the shed enough, he laid down his tools and packed up for the night, picked up the jar of Goo, he went back inside the house. Once inside he immediately placed the jar of Goo in one of his wellies that stood by the fireplace, making sure the Goo was safe by keeping it in two locations.

Assured by that, he made himself a well deserved hot mug of milk and because he was so tired he skipped his usual night time smoke and went straight to bed, and it wasn't long before he was snoring right until morning.

An Unexpected Alliance

The next morning came quickly for Mr Wilf, as it does when you've had a sound sleep, and he was up bright and early and ready for action. After consuming a hearty breakfast and getting all suited and booted, he preened his moustache and when he had finally topped himself off with a carnation in his lapel, he was set and ready to go into town.

This time however, it wasn't to go shopping or to buy a newspaper, this time he was on a mission and that mission was to find old Mr Snooby!

Mr Wilf made haste and he was very busy in his mind as he went, thinking over and over what he was going to say to Mr Snooby when he came across him.

On his journey through the town he happened to spot Sgt Grimper outside the local supermarket and he could see he was stood talking to two security guards who looked like they had just apprehended a couple of young men for shoplifting.

When Mr Wilf walked past the scene he couldn't help but overhear the Grimp's conversation, he was pleading with the store security guards to give the culprits a job for the day and in return if they did a good days work for free, there would

153

be no need to press charges and he was trying to get them to agree.

No matter how intriguing the situation was to Mr Wilf, he was still on a mission and possibly one to save the world! So he didn't bother to hang around to see the outcome, he had bigger concerns on his mind and he just carried on his way visiting each of Mr Snooby's usual haunts trying to find him. He wasn't long in the finding though, when he spotted him sat in a window seat in a cafe at the edge of town. This was where Mr Wilf expected he might be because the prices were a bit cheaper there and it looked like he was eating a full English breakfast.

Mr Wilf went inside to get a cup of tea and on turning around from the counter to see where he could sit he saw that Mr Snooby was already beckoning him to a chair to sit beside him, which Mr Wilf was half expecting he would do.

"Good morning," said Mr Wilf

"Good morning to you sir," replied Mr Snooby adding, "I haven't seen you in here before."

"Ah well Mr Snooby, that's because I've never been in here before, I'm only in here now because I've been looking for you," said Mr Wilf intriguingly.

Mr Snooby was now all ears and he leant closer to Mr Wilf, almost into a huddle keen to learn more.

"Go on," he said, practically slavering at the mouth with eager anticipation.

"Well Mr Snooby it seems you are right." said Mr Wilf pausing to look left and right, just like Mr Snooby had done outside the town hall,

"I got kidnapped by Aliens yesterday." On hearing this fantastic news Mr Snooby was practically jumping up and down in his seat eager to learn more, and taking a firm grip of Mr Wilf's arm he urged him on. "Go on, go on," he said impatiently. Which left Mr Wilf no choice now but to tell him everything he knew, and that's exactly what he did, even about Chase Me Chase Me being his invention and it also being responsible for kicking him up the arse and bending his gun around a tree, and it not being the Aliens.

By the time Mr Wilf had finished telling his whole story to Mr Snooby he knew as much as Mr Wilf did himself... Well, except about the Goo that is, Mr Wilf kept that a secret for the moment for security reasons.

Now they were both armed with much the same information, they then began to focus the rest of their discussion on a strategy to inform the public.

Several cups of tea and a couple of chip butties later it became abundantly clear to them both what their real predicament was, in realizing that no matter what they told anyone no one would believe them, especially after Mr Snooby's grand debut on live TV the other night, no one would take him seriously ever again. As for Mr Wilf, although he was a pillar of the community, they both agreed that without any real evidence or proof there was no point in him making himself look a fool in public either.

None the less they had to come up with an idea and quick. The trouble was they had been talking all day and come up with zero ideas, and now it was getting time for the cafe to close. So in desperation to get something done they decided to continue their urgent discussions elsewhere. The pub was totally out of the question because it would be far too busy, and besides Mr Snooby definitely wouldn't want to go back there again for obvious reasons. So their only other option and made at Mr Wilf's suggestion was to go up to his house instead, where he could at least relax in his chair and he was sure that between them both they could formulate a strategy to warn the public of a possible full scale Alien invasion of the Earth!

A Triple Alliance

So that being decided, the pair then set off at a hurried pace and without a moment to spare towards Mr Wilf's home. A little further into that journey and nearing the town center, Mr Wilf had another brainstorm that gave him a brilliant idea. Realizing that the Grimp might be still around town and knowing that he was still affected by the Goo, he might actually be of some use to them, so he decided to look for him on the way home.

It wasn't long before they found the Grimp who was now stood on the market square where he was handing out flowers to anyone who passed by. He was peeling them from a big bunch that was tucked under his armpit and was telling people it was a new police initiative to be nice to the public!

"Sgt Grimper, Sgt Grimper," Mr Wilf shouted to get his attention. On the Grimp hearing his call he came straight over to see what they wanted, and still wearing the same big grin on his face too, when he said.

"Hello, hello, what's all this then?" but in a comedy policeman's voice, and then he suddenly burst into laughter as though it was hilarious.

"Sgt Grimper, can you help us, we need to find

something out and we could use your help."

"Of course," replied the Grimp. "If there is anything you want you only have to ask."

So after a short explanation of sorts, Mr Wilf told him that he needed to check something out that he had found at his home, and the Grimp was more than happy to oblige his request.

Now all three of them set off heading towards Mr Wilf's home.

All the while Mr Wilf was still trying to figure out what he was going to do when they got there. By the time they arrived at his front gate, he had something in mind.

Instead of taking the pair into the house as they expected, he whisked them around to the rear garden and straight to his shed where he pointed out to them both the White Goo substance that glistened and glowed in the dark.

"What do you reckon that is then?" said Mr Wilf, pointing to the giant slug-like trail glowing on the shed wall and going into the bottle garden. However, when the Grimp stepped nearer towards it, Mr Wilf purposely held Mr Snooby back and gave him a knowing wink at the same time.

The Grimp leant curiously closer to take a better look and he couldn't resist touching it and smearing it through his fingers trying to see what it was made of.

Mr Wilf knew the Grimp would do exactly this

even knowing the Goo's effect on people, but he said nothing.

Mr Snooby was a mere spectator at this point, he was just as baffled as the Grimp was, and just watched on with Mr Wilf as the Grimp got himself plastered in the stuff while doing his investigating.

It wasn't very long before the Grimp began to feel a little weird and wobbly and started swaying about with the effect of the Goo, just like Mr Wilf had anticipated, so he made sure he was close to hand to catch him and sit him on the shed floor.

Mr Snooby was in awe, he didn't have a clue what was going on, but Mr Wilf did, he knew exactly what he was doing, he had made the calculation that if he could get the Grimp to remember the important message he obviously had forgotten from the other night, then all his questions might be answered, and if it took another dose of Goo on the Grimp to do it... then it had to be done, and anyway what harm could it do he thought?

The Grimp was now sat on the shed floor and he was becoming more spaced-out by the second, and this was when Mr Wilf took the opportunity to ask the question.

"Sgt Grimper, do you remember the other night at my house? You told me you had a very important message to tell me, do you remember what it was?"

The Grimp's face strained and with a wrinkled

brow he closed his eyes and mouth to think.

"What was it" repeated Mr Wilf practically browbeating him to answer. Then all of a sudden the Grimp's eyes sprang wide open and the grin returned to his face, and he said,

"I remember, I remember."

"Good, good, now what is it you remember" demanded Mr Wilf pressing him for an answer. Mr Snooby still hadn't a clue what was going on, yet he sensed the situation dictated he took a hold of the Grimp's hand for reassurance, because he was also wanted to hear what the important message too.

Only then to hear the Grimp say in a low soft voice making them both strain to hear, "Yes, yes, I've got it "

Then all of a sudden at the top of his voice he just blurted it out, "WHATEVER YOU DO, DON'T MESS WITH THE GOO!", and then just as sudden he fainted.

Mr Wilf looked at Mr Snooby in total surprise, he wasn't expecting that all. He jumped to his feet and ran out from the shed and straight over to the water butt, then came running back with a dripping wet flannel, and began scrubbing the white glowing substance off the Grimp as quickly as he could.

No sooner had he finished washing every last bit of it off, the Grimp started to come back around, and within only moments he had returned back to something like normal. Well... at least back to what he was like in the market place anyway.

Mr Wilf now felt it was his duty to disclose to them both what he knew about the Goo and why he had built a fortress to protect it, and because he didn't know why it needed protecting, he left that to both Snubbers and the Grimp to try and figure that out.

The trouble was it took so long in the explaining, it was around midnight by the time he had got done, but none of them were any wiser to what the Goo was all about? Now all three of them were completely exhausted and too tired to go on. So Mr Wilf made the suggestion to the other two, that if they weren't bothered about going home they could both sleep over at his house and pick up the conversation again over breakfast in the morning. To which they both agreed.

The Grimp was already on nights so it didn't matter to him at all, but surprisingly old Mr Snooby had to ring his mum up for permission first. After that being settled Mr Wilf made them each a hot mug of milk and afterwards they all decided to turn in for the night to have a nice peaceful sleep... or so they thought...

It wasn't long before all three were snoozing their heads off in their beds, but it wasn't long into the night either when strange things began to happen. Firstly when Mr Snooby, who being a light sleeper, was awoken by a buzzing sound that was coming from outside.

This happened to be a very familiar sound to old Mr Snooby that he had heard many times before and usually when UFOs were about! He quickly jumped out of bed to investigate by going over to the window to have a peak outside.

After parting the curtains he immediately saw some kind of bright searchlight coming down from the sky and it was scanning in Mr Wilf's back garden, so he ran in to the other bedrooms to wake the pair up.

Mr Wilf was easy to wake, he jumped out of bed straight away with no fuss at all, but trying to wake up Sgt Grimper... and him being ex-special forces, he nearly karate-chopped the pair of them to death mistaking them for the enemy trying to sneak up on him in the jungle again.

Eventually convincing the Grimp who they were, they all ventured downstairs putting their clothes on as they went. The kitchen fire was bright so there was no need to turn on the light, and besides they didn't want to signal what they were going to do to whoever was outside.

Mr Wilf picked up his trusty walking stick from behind the kitchen door and the Grimp chose a large iron poker from the fire place, which left Mr Snooby the privilege of carrying a big flash light torch. When they were all ready they crept to the back door, then whispering quietly Mr Wilf laid out the plan, and seeing as he was an old hand at these sort of things, the plan he came up with was to go bursting out into the garden on the count of three!

He began the count. One... two... and on three, they all went charging out the door screaming "ARGHHHHHHH" at the top of their voices and waving their makeshift weapons and arms about in the air as they did... But the lights had gone, it was pitch black outside, they could barely see their hands in front of their faces.

"That's funny," said Mr Wilf, "there's no street lights on." Although his house was on the edge of town he lived on a hill and they could see that the power was off everywhere, there wasn't a light to be seen in Normantofts, just total darkness. So the three went back inside to check the power there, but Mr Wilf's electricity was off too, and funnily enough the first thing on his mind was that all the shopping in the freezer was going to spoil. "A whole month's supply of food will be ruined," he moaned.

But before he could moan anymore about it, he was interrupted when they all heard a loud buzzing noise, which instigated them to run outside again to see what it was, and when they looked in the sky this time, they saw some strange lights in the near distance that looked to be heading over towards Spooker's Wood. Then they saw what looked like laser beams of light that seemed to be scanning the ground for something, and on looking up to see where those lights actually coming from, they also saw the dark silhouettes of spacecraft that were blocking out the stars as they moved across the sky. The more their eyes adjusted to the dark, the more of these craft they began to see. There was about ten of these saucer shaped UFOs in total and they all looked exactly like the one that took Mr Wilf to the Moon the other night.

"WOW," they all said in astonishment, as this fleet of craft then stopped moving and looked to be decending lower to the ground and congregating over a particular area of Spooker's Wood.

Noticing this Mr Wilf's made a quick mental calculation, and as far as he could figure they were hovering exactly over the old mine entrance, and it also occurred to him that they could be looking for Chase Me Chase Me and he might be trapped down the mine.

With this thought coming to mind it spurred Mr Wilf straight into action.

"Come on no time to lose" he said, pulling at the other two's arms encouraging them both to follow, and trusting Mr Wilf's hunch whatever it was they obediently did regardless.

Once again Mr Wilf set off into the darkness of Spooker's Wood, but this time he was accompanied by a UFO expert and the toughest cop in the county, so what could go wrong he thought?

It wasn't long before the trio were deep in the woods and near the old mine entrance where they almost straight away began to hear strange noises of activity, and the closer they got they also began to hear voices as well.

The dark sky above them was now full of large circular objects and they were now nearer to the ground, which made it essential to creep under the cover of the bushes to make sure they weren't seen from above. When they got closer to where all the activity was taking place, they had to get down even lower by crawling on their stomachs through a small grassy area so that they could sneak a peek.

On peeking through the grass they saw to their horror a group of about thirty large lizard creatures that were all standing in ranks like soldiers. They looked to be taking orders from another lizard, but this one was bigger and it had larger scales on its head than the others, and it looked like it was the boss. More surprising, there were humans there too, who seemed to be taking part in what was going on.

The trouble was none of the trio could quite

catch what they were all talking about, so they decided to slide even nearer staying as flat as they could in the long grass until they got in earshot of what was being said, but when they got as close as they dared to listen, another troop of these lizard Aliens came marching from out of the surrounding trees and the direction of the town. What was more shocking was that in their possession were about twenty of the local town's folk, who all looked to be held captive in the same Robotic trance Mr Wilf was under not too long ago. They were being marched in single file past this human character wearing a black cape, who then began smearing each one of them with a black tar-like substance on their foreheads.

As soon as he did this, each of the town's folk then fell into line with the other Aliens that were already stood in ranks.

All the while Mr Wilf was watching he was tweaking his moustache ferociously trying to get a better understanding of it all. Unfortunately before he could the situation became all too chillingly clear when this human figure head gave a command to the captive humans in the automated trance like state, to go and find two little boys, two little girls and an old man, and he was handing out descriptions to each of them.

Alarmingly to Mr Wilf's horror, this human character in black then announced that they were particularly interested in finding a certain person who was capable of building a Robot. Hearing this made the hairs prickle up on the back of Mr Wilf's neck and sent a shiver straight down his spine, because they were talking about him!

After hearing this chilling information there was no time to lose, Mr Wilf's mind was made up he had to go and try to save his grandchildren no matter what.

So he indicated to both the Grimp and Snubbers by pointing over his shoulder with his thumb and only after receiving two nods of acknowledgement they began slowly retreating backwards on all fours, keeping low as they did until they got a safe distance away.

When it was safe to stand up they had a quick discussion

"What was all that about, then?" enquired the Grimp.

"Shhh... I will explain later on the way," replied Mr Wilf, "There's no time to lose, we have to move... and fast."

So off they went with Mr Wilf leading the way at an extra hurried pace through the dense wooded thicket, but it was heavy going and very tiring , so it wasn't long before the three were getting a bit puffed out. At the first opportunity when they reached a small clearing they decided to take a short rest, and seeing as they had Mr Wilf went on to explain to them both.

"Those descriptions they gave out were of me and the grandchildren, which means we will have to go to each of their houses to warn them as soon as possible and afterwards we can all meet at mine, I have a plan, but I will tell you later." he said, adding, "come on we need to get a move on"

But the thing was, just as they were preparing to leave the clearing a big Alien Lizard suddenly jumped out from the bushes in front of them, which then went GRRRRRR, stopping Mr Wilf dead in his tracks, freezing the other two to the spot. Fortunately, just as it was going to point a wand control stick at them Mr Wilf reacted in a flash, because he had seen how these things worked before, and using his Ninja skills he quickly knocked it out of its hand with his walking stick and before the Alien knew it Mr Snooby had dazzled it with his torch, leaving the Grimp time to follow up by bashing it over the head with the iron poker, instantly sending it crumpling to the floor with one fell swoop.

The trouble was, just before this Alien hit the deck it managed to let out one final screech, and in that instant all the surrounding bushes were suddenly filled with the sound of screeching in return. It was as though these creatures had sensed what had just happened to one of their own and now that screeching was getting nearer by the second.

The sound they made was so terrifying no words were needed, all three just legged it as fast as they could and headed in the direction of the nearest place of safety, which was Mr Wilf's house where he had already built his fortress-in-the-waiting, and it was also a place where he could at least ring up the grandkids' homes and warn them, which was a start.

No matter how urgently they pressed on the direct route they had taken meant they now had to fight their way through the dense gauze and bushes until they hit a path, and although they had made some distance the screeching sound was still following them close behind. Even more worryingly, it sounded to be catching up with them as well! It was so terrifying to hear, that although the three were totally exhausted and more than ready for bed, it was enough to make them dig deeper than they had ever dug before to find that extra energy to run for their lives. To Mr Wilf's astonishment, Snubber's who previously had to be helped along by the Grimp dragging him by his collar, was now way in front leading the pack.

Luckily it wasn't too long before they reached Mr Wilf's rear garden, where he insisted the other two waited in the safety of his fortress like shed while he went indoors to use the phone. In that instant the Grimp produced his mobile which was even better, but it was no use it was dead, so Mr Wilf ran in the house to use the house phone as he had planned instead, but that was dead too, which was very strange so Mr Wilf decided to return to the shed to consult the others when all of a sudden he heard a loud commotion coming from outside. So Mr Wilf cautiously made his way to the back door to see what it was, but when he did, he saw to his absolute horror that both the Grimp and Mr Snooby were now stood on the lawn in a trance-like state and the Aliens were already rooting about in his shed. There looked to be about five in total, and to his alarm a couple of Aliens then came out of his shed carrying his bottle garden and other items that were glowing in the dark as well. No sooner had the Aliens got what they wanted, they then suddenly clomped off down the garden path taking their new captives with them, through the gate and back towards Spooker's Wood.

Mr Wilf now had to do some quick thinking... and once he had, he dashed back into the kitchen and grabbed his jar of Goo from out of his wellie and slipped it in his jacket pocket. He then went out of the front door and took George's trick bike from the garage and set off out of the gate pedaling like mad, straight down all the back alleyways towards the street where his grandchildren lived.

Luckily they didn't live too far away, and they

were near neighbours in the same street. It wasn't long before Mr Wilf was hammering on the first of the doors where he left a brief message and then onto the next house. Within a couple of minutes he had managed to arouse both of his families convincing them with a ruse that there was an emergency at Nana's house.

Believing their Granddad's story they all wasted no time at all in getting ready to leave, but there was a snag and a big one too, none of the motor vehicles would start! So Mr Wilf decided that although it was wasting more time, to tell them all about the Aliens to convince them they needed to go.

As one can imagine at this point, his family members were becoming less convinced and more worried for Granddad's sanity by the second. No matter how much the grandchildren insisted he was telling the truth, the parents were convinced that their Granddad had finally lost the plot and now were in agreement to return indoors to comfort him instead.

Fortunately for Mr Wilf, his daughter just happened to look up into the sky out of curiosity, and when she did she actually saw a UFO hovering above them.

"Wow," she said, pointing it out to everyone else, who all went "Wow" too. But the situation was about to get even worse, when they all then noticed a troop of about ten people marching up the street and walking in step like Zombie Robots heading straight towards them!

At the front of this troop was Sgt Grimper and he definitely wasn't smiling now! But wearing a very mean looking frown instead!

"QUICK! GET BACK INDOORS" yelled Mr Wilf, at the same time desperately herding his family towards George and Charlie's front door. Once inside they all started barricading the doors, using two old church pews to wedge each door closed and piled anything else they could up behind them.

"There, that should buy us some time," Granddad said, before taking the time to sit down for a few moments to take a breather. While he did he also took the opportunity to consult his moustache for guidance.

The trouble was everyone was panicking and now demanding an explanation from Granddad as to what was going on, and because he was the centre of everyone's attention he became too distracted to consult his moustache properly, and he was unable to come up with anything at all. That is until little Charlie offered his Granddad his Super-soaker saying, "We could blast them with this Granddad." Which automatically made Mr Wilf smile regardless of the given situation and he received Charlie's token suggestion gratefully, thinking it was of no use at all... but was it?

Mr Wilf's moustache tweaking must have worked after all. He jumped up to his feet and headed straight to the kitchen sink where he began filling up the Super-soaker with water as fast as he could. When George saw what his Grandad was doing he went and got his Super, super soaker from his toy box and joined the queue to fill his up too.

Mr Wilf then produced his jar of the mysterious White Goo from his coat and proceeded to put a teaspoon of it in each of the Super-soakers. No sooner he had and sensing this was going to be some kind of water fight, Charlie and Evie came running into the kitchen with a box of water balloons to join in. These were also received gratefully and hurriedly filled with diluted Goo too. No explanation was needed, they were quickly distributed equally and when everyone was armed to the teeth and ready, all that was left to do was listen and wait.

And they didn't have to wait long, when all of a sudden a really loud knocking was heard on the front door which make everyone fall silent, it went so quiet you could hear a pin drop, and now all eyes were transfixed in the direction from where that knocking sound came. Then to everyones alarm the letterbox popped open, which made everyone jump, especially when they all saw a pair of familiar eyes peering through at them, and they belonged to the Grimp! Who then in a angry deep voice said, "You've got two minutes to come out or we are coming in," then in a more sinister tone he added, "Someone wants to seeee youuuuuuuuuu, wuhu ha ha ha ha haaaarrr."

Now most people would be terrified at this point but not Granddad Wilf, he was as cool as a cucumber, he was so confident that his Goo Super-soakers would do the trick he sensed he had the upper hand for a change, and because of this he even dared to offer the Grimp a challenge back, when to everyone else's surprise he shouted,

"WELL IF YOU WANT SOME, YA BETTER COME AND GET IT THEN!"

The kids weren't fazed at all they were loving every minute of it, they couldn't wait for some action to start and they didn't have to wait long for that either. The front door suddenly came crashing off its hinges and when it fell to the floor there in its place now stood a big menacing figure instead, it was Sgt Grimper. Behind him was a small army of towns folk who were all in the same zombie state, completely blocking the doorway, and to everyone's surprise they all started snarling for some reason too.

Hearing this awful sound Mr Wilf quickly shone his torch in their direction to see exactly who was there and making the snarling noises. When the beam of light lit them, they all could see that it was Sgt Grimper who had a really evil look on his face and standing by his side were both Mr Snooby and Bill the landlord from the Dog and Ferret, and stood behind them were some other mean faced towns folk too. It was also noticeable that the one thing they all had in common besides the snarling, was that they all had black Goo dripping from their foreheads, and the one with the meanest face of all and snarling the most... was Mr Golding the milkman.

Sgt Grimper then said in a deep voice, "Are you coming peacefully, or do we have to take you by force?"

Again, Mr Wilf just stood there as cool as a cucumber, and still being able to maintain his cheery face, he then uttered those immortal words,

"Well, come and have a go if you think you're hard enough."

On hearing this reply, the whole bunch of these Zombie Robots suddenly went, "Grrrrrrrrrrrr," and began lurching towards Mr Wilf and his family with their arms and fingers outstretched, they went clomp ...clomp ...clomp all walking in step and all ready to make a grab.

No matter how scary the situation looked, Granddad Wilf was just calmly issuing instructions in a low voice to George who was standing by his side with his Super, super soaker and his artillery who were now stood behind an upturned settee, armed to the teeth with their Goo bombs at the ready, because timing was crucial to make his plan work.

"Steady... steady... hold your fire... hold your fire," he calmly said, making sure the Grimp and the rest of his zombie army got fully into the room and near enough to blast. Everyone was hanging on to their Granddad's every word with each step the zombie army made towards them.

"Steady.. steady... Hold... Hold your fire... just a little bit further... Hold your fire," he said reassuringly while waiting right until the very last moment. Just as the Grimp set foot on the opposite end of the living room rug Granddad Wilf shouted, "LET THEM HAVE IT" at the same time pulling the trigger of his super-soaker as he did, blasting the Grimp straight in the mush and stopping him dead in his tracks.

In that instant everyone opened fire and now this once-darkened room suddenly lit up with the wondrous spectacle of dozens of glowing white water balloons and crisscrossing jets of this luminous Goo flying through the air, exploding like a magical firework display as they hit their targets.

The Goo was splashing in every direction, cascading down on the zombies like a fountain and soaking them right down to their boots. Granddad and his comrades were relentless, they kept pelting and blasting furiously to make sure they got them all. The zombies didn't stand a chance, they couldn't escape the onslaught from the Goo if they tried, especially with George's Super, super-soaker skills, blasting them from every angle possible, not to mention the brilliant artillery support from behind the settee, where little Charlie was even bold enough to leave its safety, daring to go right up to a zombie and throw the Goo bombs directly in its face.

All the while the kids thought it was all just fun, they were having a great time.

Suddenly, in the mayhem of splashes and shouts of, "Have it... Eat this..." they heard the Grimp's voice cry out, "Mr Wilf... Stop it, stop it, it's me, what are you doing!" Which was a good indication that the Goo was working and a lucky thing too, because as they were running out of ammo, but no one stopped until every last Goo bomb was thrown and both Super -soakers were completely drained, just in case!

When they did, all that was left was an eerie silence as the victors stood to gaze upon the vanquished, who were now staring back at them, but no longer a pack of lethal intruders but a bunch of harmless townspeople who were absolutely soaked to the bone, glowing in the dark and didn't have a clue as to why they were there in the first place!

Then all of a sudden everyone just unexpectedly burst into laughter for no reason at all... or was there a reason? As the laughter died down it was obvious that the Grimp, Mr Snooby and the other towns people were all back to normal again. But before anyone had a chance to speak or explain anything about what was actually going on, a familiar loud buzzing sound was heard outside and it sounded like it was directly over the house.

"Shhhhh... listen... listen... out there" said Mr Snooby, so everyone went quiet to listen. The humming buzzing sound got louder and louder, and it sounded like it was getting nearer to the ground. So Bill the landlord the Grimp's brother, went to the front door to take a peek outside and no sooner he did, he came running back into the room with a look of alarm on his face.

"Quick, quick," he shouted. "There's a massive flying saucer outside and it's landed in the street and a load of Aliens are coming towards the house."

Again no words were needed – it was time for quick thinking, but there wasn't enough time for Granddad Wilf to consult his moustache and come up with a plan. Fortunately, George's mum came up with one instead, when surprisingly she ushered everyone over towards the old fireplace, where she went on to explain that the house was an old church building and when they had renovated it sometime ago they had inadvertently found an old secret escape passage that led down to the stream, also stating that although it was hundreds of years old and it hadn't been inspected for a long time, she was sure it was quite safe. Then after pressing a little button on the old oak panel in the wall it exposed a secret tunnel, to which Mr Wilf gave a quick inspection with his torch light and after checking it was ok, he said "Right, everybody in here," and everyone did as he said without any argument.

One by one they all filed into the small narrow stone passage, each taking a candle from an old box that was on the reverse of the panel, and although the candles looked ancient they lit up no problem at all.

Mr Wilf was the last man and just as he was stepping into the tunnel he suddenly heard big heavy footsteps walking over the same door that the Grimp had just barged down. So he very carefully and quietly replaced the oak panel behind him, and no sooner he had the Aliens entered into the living room and he could hear them searching around, which meant he had to stay real quiet and tread very carefully from now on, so with extra caution in mind Mr Wilf tiptoed off down the tunnel to catch the others up, but still going as fast as he could!

They were all now in single file and making their way down this old dark dripping wet narrow stone tunnel and crouching as they went, especially when they had to climb over rubble that was underfoot from small roof collapses that had occurred over the years. In spite of that they all pressed on regardless because there was definitely no going back now.

The tunnel was at least two hundred meters long which eventually came to an abrupt end, where the only way out was up a small vertical shaft leading to the surface. It was about ten feet high, leaving them no choice but to try and climb out. Luckily where ancient ladders used to be, tree roots were now hanging down to the bottom which made it so much easier for everyone to climb their way to the top.

The first to surface was Mr Snooby, who came out under a big old oak tree on the bank above the stream. The last man to scramble out of this hole in the ground was of course Mr Wilf, who was just about to make some suggestions to where they all should go, assuming they were all safe and out of danger. He was mistaken, the buzzing noise came back again and it sounded like it was coming in their direction. So now everyone was in a panic and wondering what to do next, when Sgt Grimper had a sudden flash of wisdom.

"I don't know why but I'm getting the feeling that it would be actually safer at mine or at Nana's house," he said with a mysterious look on his face. Seeing the Grimp was still all Goo'd up, Mr Wilf was quite happy to follow his inclination.

So off they all trooped as fast as they could towards Nana's, which was a bit of a journey, especially at night and with kids in tow. Fortunately, in realising the stream they were following went around the back of the Dog and Ferret, Bill the landlord had a great idea. He ran into his pub's beer garden as they passed by and dragged out a white-water dinghy that his kids played about with in the stream.

Noticing Bill's effort everyone pitched in and helped pull the dinghy into the water, where everyone began boarding it as quickly as they could. Although it was a tight fit they all managed to squeeze in, but by the time that they did the buzzing humming noise suddenly came back, and now it was nearly overhead. Leaving them no other choice but to start paddling like mad to try to outrun it, and their only chance to gain any real distance was to hit the fast white water in the stream as soon as they could to pick up more speed.

With the buzzing noise now directly above them they all began to paddle like they had never paddled before, and with shear effort they managed reach the fast water in no time at all. Although it became a typical wet and bumpy ride and everyone had to cling on to the dinghy for dear life, it was much better getting wet than being caught by the Aliens that were chasing them!

Fortunately, by the time the stream smoothed out they had managed to put some distance between themselves and the buzzing sound, and before they all knew it the dinghy was already bumping up the stream bank at the rear of Nana and Sgt Grimper's houses, where everyone quickly alighted the dinghy and dragged it up onto the bank and hid out of sight.

There they all sat in the bushes as quiet as church mice listening, and when Mr Wilf was sure that the buzzing noise had definitely gone and they were now out of danger, he whispered,

"Right then, if everyone is ready we are going to go to check on Nana firstly, but it's very important for everyone to stay as quiet as they can because we don't want to startle her".

After receiving a unanimous nod of heads, they all set off creeping silently towards Nana's house. But as they crept up her rear garden path they noticed some strange flashing lights that were coming from inside the house, and the closer they got they also began to hear some really weird noises as well?

Thinking the worst, Mr Wilf brought everyone behind him to an abrupt halt, making the "Shhhh" sound with his finger to his lips, and whispered a plan to the others.

"We don't know what might be inside, so I

suggest that we each pick up a lump of wood or something, anything you can find laying about the garden, and when we're ready, on the count of three, we will all go rushing in and no matter what is in there clobber the living daylights out of it... are you with me!" After receiving another unanimous nod of heads they all quickly searched for anything they could find.

Within seconds everyone was armed to the teeth. They had a stick, a shovel, a garden rake, half an old clothes prop and a few other rudimentary weapons that were at hand, but for some reason Charlie was holding a big dead fish by the tail he found floating in Nana's pond.

None the less Mr Wilf started the count...

"One... Two... and on three they all went charging inside yelling as loud as they could, but not all yelling the same thing at the same time.

They yelled, "ARHHHH WE'RE COMING NANA, YARRRRRRR LEAVE MY NANA ALONE," but in reality it sounded more like "YANNANARLAMMANANA".

When they all stormed into the room where the lights and noise were coming from, to everyone's surprise they saw that it was just Nana sat up late watching her brand new 100-inch TV, with the volume turned up really loud and she was watching a sci-fi movie.

The strangest thing was that when they all piled

in from behind her she didn't even notice, she was just sat happily sucking on a jammy dodger she had been dipping in hot milk. (Nana's house was fed electricity from down the valley in the next borough which wasn't affected by the power cut and everything seemed to be functioning ok!)

"NANA" everyone shouted above the din, but in doing so they nearly frightened her half to death in the process, and almost frightened her other half when she turned around to see half the town in her living room, stood staring back at her all holding makeshift weapons in their hands as well!

"Ayup... what's going off here like?" Nana demanded to know, with more than a put out look on her face and squinting furiously.

No matter that being the case, Mr Wilf left that to the others to explain because he had urgent need of the telephone, which he immediately picked up... and bingo, there was indeed a dialing tone.

So Mr Wilf proceeded to dial 9... 9... however just as he dialled the last digit the phone suddenly went dead, and thats not all, at that same moment the buzzing humming noise came back, and in that instant Nana's electricity went off too, plunging the whole house into total darkness.

So everyone went dead quiet in order to listen to the humming noise outside, which now seemed to be coming from all directions and noticeably to them all, lower to the ground.

Realizing what this meant, everyone jumped to it and pitched in to start barricading the doors as quickly as they could. It was a frantic scene but everyone just got on with it, only grunts of exhaustive effort could be heard above the now very loud humming buzzing noise coming from outside. They worked together as a team, pushing the settees against patio doors and anything they could stack against them (except the new TV of course!).

After hurriedly fortifying the house, Mr Wilf once again took the time to consult his moustache to try to come up with an idea and quickly. Although no other plan came to mind, he got the sudden inclination that he needed to hide his jar of Goo and keep it safe no matter what. So to keep it out of harm's way he took it from his jacket pocket and swiftly secreted it in the chimney breast while no one was watching.

Then taking command of the situation as he usually did, Mr Wilf went to address the others to inform them what the real predicament was by explaining that he wasn't confident about using the Goo idea this time, because something was telling him that it wouldn't work on the Aliens and their wand control sticks, and he didn't know how to combat them, so their only option now was to hold out until daylight when he was sure the Aliens wouldn't want to be seen around. No sooner had he finished explaining the situation and before anyone could say a word, all the doors and windows suddenly came crashing in, and in seconds Mr Wilf and his band where totally overwhelmed by a large group of Aliens who came bursting into the house from every which way possible!

Poor Mr Wilf and his family and friends were quickly overwhelmed by the Alien wand control sticks from every direction, they didn't know what hit them, and within a few moments they were all under Alien control and being marched out of the house in single file, and strangely enough even Nana was marching too.

Although they were all under the Alien spell, they were all still aware of their surroundings and knew exactly what was happening to them. Once outside they could plainly see that next to the houses in the adjacent field where three big spaceships with about ten Aliens standing guard outside each one.

Then a bigger Alien about a foot taller than the rest and with a lot more scales on its head emerged from one of the craft and headed straight in their direction. As it came stomping towards them it looked really mean, and as it approached the Alien that was guarding them then used the control wand stick to make the humans turn an about-face, just like soldiers in rank would do: Mr Wilf was half expecting them to make him do a salute next.

This fearsome creature then suddenly stopped directly in front of the line of its human captives, where it then began staring at them menacingly, looking them up and down each in turn.

As it did, everyone began to hear a voice but in their heads only, which very aggressively said,

"Where is the Robot... which one of you knows?" and pausing for an answer, it then turned its attention to Mr Wilf and began glaring at him intensely. So much so Mr Wilf could feel something inside his head and he got this sudden overwhelming compulsion to tell the Alien everything he knew... and he was just going to, but before he could utter a word, another spaceship arrived on the scene, it came passing really low over Nana's house roof before coming to a halt and hovering directly over the garden.

On the Aliens seeing this, it had now had their whole and undivided attention, and it was noticeable to Mr Wilf that they all looked confused, even more so when it suddenly dropped down and plonked itself on Nana's lawn. By the looks on the Alien's faces they weren't expecting that either.

As soon as the craft touched down a ramp began to lower, and as it did everyone and everything's eyes were now fixed on this ramp, as it slowly extended to the ground. No sooner it did the spacecraft's lights then came on all around, which lit the entire garden. Then a door opened at the top of its ramp exposing a bright light emanating from inside.

At first nothing happened, no one came out, there was just a silence. The Aliens looked confused at this point, especially the big boss one, which actually looked like it was scratching its head (the head scratching must be a universal thing Mr Wilf thought).

Then it made a low-pitch screechy noise to the others, who then all began advancing towards this mystery spaceship, even the ones that were guarding the other craft did too, but they all looked to be very wary and cautious as they did.

Just as the Aliens got a couple of yards from its ramp, the light that was emanating from its door was suddenly eclipsed by a large dark figure, which now cast a giant shadow the full length of the garden. This made all the Aliens stop and hesitate for a moment. The shadow of the figure then appeared to walk from out of the light and onto the ramp. As it did the shadow grew smaller but the glare from the light behind got bigger, and it was still masking whoever it was out.

All of a sudden the lights on the craft went completely out, plunging the garden once again into total darkness, and just as suddenly as the lights went out, they all came back on again, but this time to reveal the identity of the mysterious occupant from within.

And there for all to see standing at the top of the ramp as bold as ever with that big silly grin on his face and a Cuban cigar hanging out of his mouth, was Chase Me Chase Me!

Who surprisingly began rubbing his leathery hands together and shaking with laughter at the same time (like a cartoon villain with a cunning plan). He then suddenly produced one of the Alien wand sticks from under his armpit and began baton-twirling it from one hand to the other, and in his own familiar Robot voice, he then shouted directly to Mr Wilf,

"AYUP MR WILFERS, I'LL BE WITH YOU IN A MO, JUST GIVE ME TWO TICKS!" this was followed by a knowing wink, as he did.

At that very moment all the Aliens suddenly began slowly advancing towards Chase Me Chase Me, but now all screeching with excitement as though sensing an easy victory, as he stood there all alone.

They lurched forward with their four-clawed fingered hands outstretched and ready to grab a hold of the Robot they had been so keen on capturing all of this time.

But as they all neared the bottom of the ramp, Chase Me Chase Me pointed the wand control stick at his human friends, just as the first Aliens foot touched the bottom of the ramp, and set them free from the Alien's spell.

Surprisingly then, he flung his hand in the air and began mimicking a big fight night presenter making his announcement, echoes and all.

"LETS GET READY TO RUMBLE!"

Hearing this the Aliens froze on the spot, as though mesmerized and wondering what was coming next. They didn't have to wait long to find that out. When on the last echo of "RUMBLE," and to everyone's absolute surprise, especially the Aliens, about fifty or more other Chase Me Chase Me's came bursting out from behind him, and in a flash they had completely filled the entire ramp surrounding their leader in a solid wall of Robot protection.

The Aliens were now in a state of alarm and stood practically open mouthed in shock, not only were they outnumbered, but it was plain to see that these were no ordinary Chase Me Chase Me's. They were bigger and looked more fearsome, and built more like fighting Robots, rather than being made from old converted slot machines and having soft leathery hands and big circus boots, they all had brass knuckledusters across their fingers and wore steel toe cappers instead!

The Aliens couldn't believe their eyes, which nearly popped out of their heads, and they also made the "URHHHHHHH" sound at the same time (which must be another universal thing when you're deffo not expecting something), and before the boss Alien leader could offer any direction to

190

the others, it was only to be distracted once again by the sound of Chase Me Chase Me's voice as he was raised aloft by fellow Robots in a seated position like he was in a Emperor's chair, whilst making the sarcastic remark, "How do you like these apples then?" and without waiting for a response, he then very skillfully flicked his cigar from his hand straight into his mouth and gave the command, "GO GET EM BOYS!"

In a instant his army of fighting Chase Me Chase Me's sprang straight into action, they went diving off the ramp straight into their enemy with flying kicks, head butts and good old school wind milling and booting as they went.

The Aliens didn't know what hit them, their wand control sticks and claws were useless on these new Chase Me Chase Me's, they had no effect on them at all, and although the Aliens were mega strong they were no match for this new army of tough fighting Robots, they were getting whooped good style!

Not only were the Aliens getting clobbered from the front by all the Chase Me Chase Me's, but they were also getting equally clobbered from the rear too, by Mr Wilf and his army of now very angry townspeople demanding retribution from their would-be captors.

All who were able wasted no time at all in rolling up their sleeves and getting stuck into the fray as best they could and with anything they could lay their hands on too. The Aliens were getting jabbed by bamboo canes from Nana's rose bushes and hit over the head with every garden implement you could think of. Those who had nothing to hand helped to impede the Aliens by either pulling on their tails or stamping on their toes.

Even Nana managed to get into the fight by clinging onto the big Alien's leg, where she had sunk her brand-new set of screw-in dentures into its thigh and locked on, and no matter how much the big Alien squealed and desperately tried to shake her off, it couldn't because George was keeping it busy pelting it from an inexhaustible stockpile of garden ornaments, and if that wasn't enough, it could hardly see from being blasted in its mush by Evie and Molly Sue who were having fun with the garden hosepipe, doing their little bit too.

As one garden gnome after another bounced off its head, Nana held on for dear life. All the while Mr Wilf and the Grimp bravely battled to Nana's aid, and each Alien they came upon they got a taste of a bare-knuckle sandwich as they went, and the Aliens didn't like this at all! They were now squealing like little girls as their ribs got pummeled and lizard chins got upper-cutted from left to right. There was Alien teeth and snot flying everywhere, and it wasn't too long before the fearsome screeching noises these creatures once made were now reduced to just that of painful moans and groans instead. They were totally outnumbered and outmatched by superior forces and they were getting their arses kicked good and proper.

The battle had become so one-sided that some of the Chase Me Chase Me's even had time to swing a couple of the Aliens around by their tails and bang their heads together like they were playing conquers (conkers)... just for fun. As each of the Aliens fell their bodies were piled up everywhere, until finally there was only one left standing, which was the big boss one with the scaly head. There it stood all on its own, completely surrounded by this formidable army of Chase Me Chase Me's and a bunch of angry town folk wanting some payback.

Surprisingly, although it was totally trapped and outnumbered, it crouched down and it was maneuvering in its encirclement and snarling in defiance, obviously showing it was ready to put up a good fight. It was certainly giving a good impression it wasn't going to go down easily.

So all eyes automatically searched for Chase Me Chase Me to see what to do next, and to everyone's astonishment, he was sitting at the top of the spaceship's ramp where he had been taking it easy, smoking one of Nana's cigars and reading a comic all the while, and it was only now that he had got everyone's attention focused in his direction, did he decide to get up off his backside to participate.

Chase Me Chase Me rose to his feet but taking the time to carefully fold up his comic and tuck it under his arm, stubbed his cigar out on the side of the spaceship, and then he just casually walked to the edge of the ramp, where everyone was expecing him to speak. In anticipation of what he was about to say Chase Me Chase Me then clasped his hands and began rubbing them together (as you would when you're looking forward to doing something) and almost like making an announcement he then said, "I reckon this calls for a double head crunch." And raising his voice he directly shouted, "DON'T YA THINK SO MR WILF?" nodding to him has he did.

Mr Wilf being a bit of a Ninja knew exactly what Chase Me Chase Me meant, quickly acknowledging him back with the old fashioned nod and a wink. The pair then mysteriously proceeded to take backwards steps as though to take a run up, then on coming to a halt both at the ready, Chase Me Chase Me shouted, "HERE WE COME MR ALIEN!" On that note they set off running at the same time, each taking a synchronized leap through the air, Chase Me Chase Me from the top of the spaceships ramp and Mr Wilf from a pile of dead Aliens, both using deadly flying kicks.

In that very instant the big Alien was taking

a peek over the heads of the townspeople and fighting robots encircling it, trying to see what all the shouting was all about. But before he could see anything its head suddenly got crunched from each side by Mr Wilf's and Chase Me Chase Me's feet meeting together mid-air, heel to heel, squashing the Aliens head.

The Aliens head went crunch, and its eyes actually popped out on stalks before dangling down its face, it then let out one last death curdling screech and went crumpling in a big heap to the ground.

And where this fearsome creature once stood now only remained a twitching hulk, blowing green snot bubbles from its nostrils, and as the last remnants of it life departed from it's huge Alien body, it did so through its long lizard forked tongue that wriggled from side to side in the dirt, which made a "sthizzle" sound as it did.

However, before its tongue could do one more sthizzle, little Charlie was too impatient and he couldn't wait any longer for it to expire. He suddenly pulled from his mothers grip, and screaming, "EAT THIS MR LIZZARD MAN" he splattered it straight in its fizzer (face) with his dead fish and silenced it once and for all. Which earned him a instantaneous big cheer of "HURRAH" from everyone, followed by another big round of ... "HURRAH FOR CHARLIE, HURRAH

FOR CHASE ME CHASE ME, HURRAH FOR MR WILF, HURRAH FOR NANA, HURRAH FOR GEORGE," right down to "HURRRAH FOR REG THE VEG", the local green grocer.

Unfortunately their celebrations were cut short when they were suddenly interrupted by a loud bellowing voice that was heard coming from a lit upstairs window in the Grimp's house, where a furious Mrs Grimper had put her head outside still wearing her curlers and screaming angrily in their direction.

"IS THAT YOU OUT THERE RUPERT? WHAT THE HELL IS GOING ON, HAVE YOU BEEN ON THAT CIDER AGAIN? I HEARD YOUR VOICE I KNOW YOUR THERE, YOU'RE FOR IT WHEN YOU GET IN, JUST YOU WAIT."

Then as suddenly as she had appeared, she disappeared, slamming the window behind her and turning off the light!

Under normal circumstances this would have been absolutely hilarious, not only did Mrs G fail to notice all the chaos in her neighbour's garden, but what was even more amazing, was the fact she had just inadvertently told half the town the Grimp's big secret: his real name! Surprisingly no one laughed at all, everyone was either too traumatized from the control wand sticks or too battle-weary to even care. Rupert wasn't bothered either!!

But the thing was, that when everyone looked around to see what Mrs G failed to see, four spaceship's, an army of robots, a pile of dead Aliens and half the town stood in Nana's back garden that now looked like a battlefield, then came the sudden realization of the immensity of what had just actually taken place, so in those moments taking all this in, there came a peaceful silence...

However before the dust had chance to settle or the last leaf fall to the ground, that silence was broken by a mighty clap of Chase Me Chase Me's hands, which nearly made everyone jump out of their skins, when he decided it was time to get moving and said

"Right, come on boys lets snap to it, it's time to get busy"

In that instant his army of fighting robots once again activated to their given task and sprang straight into action, but not for a fight this time but to tidy up Nana's garden instead. They firstly began by dragging all the dead Aliens onto each of the spaceships, as they were the proud owners of four spacecraft now, and while most of the Robots did just that, Chase Me Chase Me gave a few others the task of fixing up Nana's house.

When he had finished dishing out orders to his minions, he then turned his attention to his friends and the towns people, and seeing that they were gathered together on the patio patiently awaiting his presence, Chase Me Chase Me wasted no time in making his way over to officially meet them all. He came clomping over with the same big silly grin on his face and with his telescopic arms outstretched, the first person he approached was of course Mr Wilf.

"Put it there Dad" he said, and shook his hand, and before Mr Wilf could even respond to what he just called him, Chase Me Chase Me had relinquished his grip and turned to address everyone else

"Well, I think it's about time we all had a little chat don't you agree?" and surprisingly everyone replied by punching the air at the same time, to cries of "Yeah." On that positive response, Chase Me Chase Me quickly scooped up the two little girls, Evie and Molly onto his shoulders and with George and Charlie close by his side he led the way towards the house, and without question everyone obediently followed from behind.

Once inside everyone assembled in the main living room because it was the least messy, and they all sat in a huddle around Chase Me Chase Me's feet, where he took command of the great armchair that resided next to the fireplace, all sat quietly awaiting to hear him speak.

Mr Wilf felt inclined to do what everyone else was doing but he wasn't as star struck as the rest, and he couldn't help notice that no one else seemed to be fazed about anything that had just happened. Not even the fact they were now all waiting to hear from a strange looking robot with a big silly grin on its face that was made from amusement arcade parts that he had knocked up in his shed. The weird thing was that they we're all just sat there with the same silly grins on their faces too!

When everyone was ready Chase Me Chase Me began to speak in his given voice and everyone was listening with bated breath, ready to hang on every word uttered from his robot mouth.

"So, what you all need to know I haven't got time to tell you in full, because it will soon be daylight and we will have to go. Most of you already understand the essence of what I'm about to say because I can see you have been covered in the White Goo. The trouble is you have also been under the spell of the Aliens, and because of that you might not remember much of this tomorrow, so in anticipation of this I have made you all some instructions to follow."

"As regards to you Dad," he said directly looking at Mr Wilf, who now had raised eyebrows and nudged a little closer eager to hear more. "Here's the quick explanation, but not all the answers for now, but here goes anyway!"

"You know that bottle garden you and your dear wife cultured into a beautiful miniature paradise, which you both loved and cherished together all those years to the point you both even fantasized about living in it one day?"

"Yes," said Mr Wilf,

"Well, there came a time after sadly when you could no longer bring yourself to look upon it without being reminded of your dear wife Rose, so you decided to put it in your shed out of sight! When the garden inside died you then used it to catch the leak from the roof which flooded over in every rain storm with fresh water, and when the Sun's rays sparkled through the optics of the glass it separated the exact light prism for it to create life. This life force seeped out time and time again, which eventually reached and penetrated the cardboard boxes where you stored your power cells which then corroded and the Goo was able to make its connection! That's how, and why Dad... I became me, I wasn't your brilliant idea, all your ideas came directly from the Goo."

"But how, but how?" interrupted Mr Wilf.
Chase Me Chase Me went on to explain.

"Well that's easy! The Goo is microscopically everywhere in your shed, every time you went in your shed tinkering you inadvertently touched or breathed in some Goo. It isn't your moustache that gives you all your ideas and connects you to the universe! It's the Goo, trust me it's the Goo which manifested me through you."

200

"So you're saying none of my ideas were mine at all, and I did nothing?" interjected Mr Wilf.

"No... no Mr Wilf you did much much more, your love became the catalyst that helped to create the exact environment to allow the White Goo to physically manifest itself outside the human body!"

Mr Wilf just sat there with his finger in his mouth in awe, still trying to figure it out. So Chase Me Chase Me gave him another clue:

"Everyone good and kind and caring has it!"

But before he could quite get it just about everyone who was still Goo'd up impatiently decided to spell it out for him and loudly too,

"LOVE MR WILF... LOVE... YOU GREW SOME LOVE."

At that very moment Mr Wilf suddenly remembered the feeling he got when he had the Goo on his hands from the slimy power cell in the garden, and putting two and two together in his mind, he began to spell out his understanding by using each of his fingers for every point he made.

"So your saying that the love that both me and my Rose put into our bottle garden was somehow preserved, then transmuted into some kind of life through light... and this Goo is love?"

"Yup, that's about nailed it Hubert," Chase Me Chase Me said, at the same time jumping to his feet, adding "Look folks, I've got to get a move on now, the Sun will be rising soon and we still need to dump these dead Aliens in a swamp somewhere and before daylight, because your neighbours will be up soon and we can't be seen around."

"But... but wait, you haven't told us why the Aliens want the Goo," interrupted Mr Wilf, which was also equally murmured by everyone else wanting to know the same too. "Yeah tell us tell us why" they all repeated.

This made Chase Me Chase Me pause for a moment, then smacking his hand on his head, he then said, "Phew silly me, that reminds me I almost forgot"

He then opened up his chest panel and pulled out a stack of booklets which he gave to Mr Wilf to hand out. On first inspection of the front cover of this booklet in bold letters it read, The Gooble, and underneath in small script it also read,

"The handbook guide to all that is good!"

Before Mr Wilf or anyone else could even peruse or question these writings, Chase Me Chase Me had set off again, saying, "Sorry, I've really got to go now" and all to a hail of cries of "Please don't go Chase Me Chase Me," coming from all of the kids, and "But where will you go?" from just about everyone else. Someone even shouted,

"You can stop at mine if ya likes."

Hearing their heartfelt pleas it made the Robot stop in his tracks and slowly turn around to speak, but this time in a much softer voice,.. "I'm sorry we really have to go now, but we will try to come back and I promise we will try to keep an eye out for you all if you need our help."

"Help?" everyone puzzled, as Chase Me Chase Me went on to say,

"Help against the Aliens, now they have taken our White Goo we will be vastly outnumbered until we can find some more, so we will have to lay low for a while," he also added, "but beware, the Aliens are the guardians of the evil Black Goo and this is inside people too, and although they are many and you here are only few, don't worry there are billions of other good people in the world, you're not alone, so use the handbook to spread the word of the White Goo as much as you can, and when everyone knows the truth the Aliens can't come back."

On that note Chase Me Chase Me again turned to leave the room, but this time it was very noticeable to all, his head was down low and his Robot chin was practically on his chest, and instead of his usual grin, he almost looked sad-like in the face as he slowly walked towards the patio door.

However, barely before he could get one of his big daft boots outside he heard the voice of Mr Wilf say, "Well how much of this Goo do you think you would need then?"

This made Chase Me Chase Me stop and pause for a moment, but then on hearing Mr Wilf also say "Do you think this might be enough?" the

Robot suddenly spun around on the spot, just in time to see Mr Wilf retrieving his hand from the chimney breast holding a large glass pickle jar full to the brim with the glowing White Goo.

Seeing this wonderful sight, Chase Me Chase Me lit up with all his bells ringing, he made every sound you would hear in an amusement arcade and immediately went clomping straight over to Mr Wilf and picked him up off the floor to give him the biggest hug in the world, and began spinning him around the room like a whirling dervish in sheer delight.

No sooner had these joyful shenanigans come to an end, Chase Me Chase Me put a now very dizzy Mr Wilf down on the deck and after doing so he took immediate possession of the jar of Goo from the mantelpiece above the fire, and holding it high for all to see, he said "Right come on everyone follow me" and still holding the jar of Goo aloft he hurriedly made his way outside, with everyone following from behind.

Once in the garden, a now very happy Chase Me Chase Me suddenly ran straight to the top of his spaceship ramp to address his faithful troops – who were already in line, all jobs done and awaiting orders. Where Chase Me Chase Me then exclaimed for all to hear:

"NOW WE HAVE THE MEANS TO BUILD A THOUSAND CHASE ME CHASE ME'S, AND IN NO

TIME AT ALL WE CAN BE READY TO KICK SOME MOON ALIEN ARSE, DO YOU AGREE BOYS!"

Surprisingly they all answered, "YOU CAN BET YA BOOTS WE DO... YES SIR... CHASSEROO... SIR!" And on that resounding reply the army of fighting Robots instantly activated and set off marching out of their ranks in four columns and boarded each of the individual spacecraft and went inside.

Now leaving Chase Me Chase Me standing alone at the top of his spaceship ramp to say his very own goodbye.

But to everyone's surprise, instead of receiving the heartfelt farewell they expected, he just clasped his hands together and said,

"Well I guess that's everything sorted now, so I best be getting off before people begin to arise, but don't forget to read the Gooble and everything will work out just dandy, so cheery-bye everybody, catch ya later," instead.

Without any further ado he turned around on the spot and quickly clomped off inside the spaceship. In that instant the door closed behind him, and all four of the spaceship's ramps began to retract, and no sooner they did, all four spacecraft engines suddenly fired up at once.

The sound was so powerful that the ground shook and vibrated right through everyone's bodies, and when the noise increased to making that familiar buzzing noise, just like when a washing machine was building up to its fast spin, it created a gravity field that was now making everyone's hair stand on end. All the dead leaves and garden debris began swirling around in the air, even the kids had to be held down by their parents, but still the four spaceship remained motionless? So sensing what the problem was Mr Wilf guided everyone further back towards the house for safety, and no sooner he did, it was only then that the four spacecraft began to slowly rise up from the ground, which then in unison slowly accelerated away, buzzing off into the distant heavens, leaving everyone waving silently at four little dots in the sky.

In those final moments of Chase Me Chase Me's departure, Nana, who had disappeared for a while suddenly came speeding from out the living room on her mobility scooter straight out onto the patio, but going so fast it was only through her skills at doing emergency front-wheel stoppies that she narrowly avoided knocking everyone over. She then jumped straight off her scooter and demanded at the top of her voice,

"Where is he, has he gone, has he gone, he's never gone without cutting my trees... has he... the little sod?"

Miraculously in that very instant one of the craft which was now just a mere dot of light in the night sky, suddenly broke out from its formation and came whizzing back towards them at a tremendous speed. After it shot past it then circled around again and dropped to a very low altitude, then it came skimming back again just above Nana's and the Grimp's rooftops, and in one swoop it chopped the tops off Nana's trees as it passed by. After doing so, it then went straight up vertically, did a couple of loop the loops, to which everyone went "Woooooooooooo" as it did, before shooting off again in the same direction as the other three spacecraft, and within a blink of the eye it too had disappeared into the blackness of space.

Which under normal circumstances would have called for a massive round of cheers from everyone, despite evoking the wrath of Mrs G the monster from next door, but surprisingly no one raised a cheer at all, not even a half-suppressed one, instead everyone was just left in silence staring vacantly at the now empty space where Chase Me Chase Me used to be. Although his speedy departure was an amazing and spectacular sight to see, it was quickly over shadowed by the sudden realization that they were now indeed all on their own.

In those few moments contemplating that very thought, their feelings were more of a sadness rather than ones of joy on seeing their dear friends go, so there they remained on Nana's patio for a while longer, just staring up into the deepness of space trying to take it all in.

Fortunately those feelings of sadness quickly faded into insignificance when the first blink of the morning Sun eclipsed the horizon announcing the start of a new day. Sending its warm welcoming rays of light over the tops of distant landscapes, like a laser beam of hope piercing the darkness, straight into the optic nerve of the eye to instantaneously remind them all how beautiful the planet Earth is.

They were also reminded of what Chase Me Chase Me had told them, that they were not all on their own and they never will be. With those comforting thoughts combined with the coming safety that daylight brings their hearts were once again reinvigorated, leaving them now in a state of absolute wonderment about all that had happened.

As the Sun rose higher in the sky, all that was left to do now was to go home and to bed, and that's what they did. Each clutching their given Goobles they said their zombie tired goodbyes to one another, and after promising to meet in the following days they then all peeled off home.

Nana wasn't tired at all, she got busy in the kitchen making breakfast and chip-butties for anyone who wanted one, while the parents got the camp beds out and unfolded the bed settees to quickly turn the whole occasion into a sleepover for the kids. When everyone was fed and Nana had tidied up the dishes, it was time for bed.

Finally leaving Mr Wilf and Mr Snooby to get settled down at the kitchen table to study the small booklet that Chase Me Chase Me had left them to read, but not before the Grimp came bursting into the kitchen with three jugs of cider and after dishing them out equally, he said,

"Well, if I'm in bother with the missus, I might as well do something to get in bother for."

So after a clink of jugs the trio sat eating chip buttie's, glugging cider and reading the GOOBLE!

On first inspection of the Gooble it was plain to see the booklet was crudely made from pieces of A4 paper cut in half, folded into quarters and stapled in the middle.

Opening the first page it read: The Gooble by Chase Me Chase Me.

Declaration: I Am Chase Me Chase Me, product of Hubert and Rose Wilf and the White Goo.

(I AM) a manifestation of pure love, here to help redress the balance between good and evil and to reset the natural equilibrium of the Earth.

Introduction: This handbook was compiled for the use of all humans of good heart throughout the whole world to guide them through the coming battles against the dark forces of evil that wish to conquer the Earth and enslave mankind. The Gooble is aptly named giving reference to the good white Goo, and the very befitting Bible passage: Ephesians 6:12, KJV: "For we wrestle not against flesh and blood, but against principalities, against powers, against the rulers of the darkness of this world, against spiritual wickedness in high places."

Glossary of terms:

White Goo = Pure Love, truth and light

Black Goo = Pure Evil, darkness and deceit

The Alien dark forces are the offspring and protectors of the black Goo who have stayed hidden in the shadows working tirelessly throughout the ages to enslave mankind, and now with help from human conspirators the time is near when they want to rule out in the open as your Gods. To counteract this there is a great awakening in the hearts of all the good people throughout the whole world (The white Goo) which cannot be stopped.

Although that being the case, the dark forces will search relentlessly day and night to try to snuff out the light of the White Goo.

Mr Wilf was chosen because he is pure of heart, Normantofts because it is in the heart of Yorkshire, the very same birthplace of a great man who not so many years ago led the campaign for the abolition of slavery! And what better place is there to make a stand than in one that is affectionately known to us all as Gods county!

The Plan To Save The World

To all people of the world of good heart, you must unite together regardless of race, skin or eye colour, national flag, religion, politics (red team/blue team) as ONE! Together as One stand under the same banner of Truth, Liberty and Justice, and a banner that also symbolizes the transparency of that movement, by using the purest element that exists and sustains life here on Earth and one that no man can set asunder, and that my friends is Water!

Since a banner cannot be made of water? The only other thing that is clear, and is practically in every household in the world is?... a piece of clear polythene, that you could put on a stick and wave like a flag, it doesn't even have to be square.

When this grand awakening comes you will see billions of people around the world marching to reject this evil and they will all be waving their polythene flags.

So that being said it's now up to you! It can only happen if the message is spread by letting everyone know about Mr Wilf's story and the plan. More importantly put it into a form of children's literature to inform the kids too, because don't forget they will be your leaders of tomorrow's new.

In the meantime I and my trusty band of fighting Robots will be helping others around the planet in many different ways, so until we meet again, all we can ask is for you to do your very best to spread the word.

Cheerie-bye signed CMCM.
p.s. Pretty please with bells on.
Do you like the sketch of me?

Although there wasn't much in text to read, its contents spoke volumes to Hubert, Rupert and Snubbers, but it was far too much to digest after all they had been through that day, not to mention the cider they had glugged. By the time they had scrutinized each page their eyes were too tired to study anymore, they were so worn out they could have slept on Mrs Spingle's washing line. So it wasn't long before the three were slumped where they were sat face down, snoring in unison and drooling on the kitchen table, each still clutching their crumpled Gooble's as they slept.

As day time came for the rest of the inhabitants of Normantofts it was business as usual. Everyone went about their daily routines doing what they normally did: going to work, getting the children ready for school, hurrying for a bus...Mr Fabooni put out his morning papers as he did every day. Everything was normal to them, all totally unaware of what had taken place while they slept safely in their beds. They didn't have the slightest inclination of the epic battle that was fought in their very own town and practically on their own doorsteps, nor did they know of the small group of townspeople who fought so bravely, standing shoulder to shoulder alongside an army of Robots against a fearsome foe to save the planet Earth in their name. And still to this day only a handful people do know.

And now you have read Mr Wilf's story, you know. So it's up to you to keep spreading the word of the Goo until everyone knows, and if a time comes when the Aliens come back you will have two choices: you will either be with the Black or the White Goo.

I know which side I'm on. Do you?

The End

Nemo Vir Est Qui Mundum Non Reddat Melorium

What man is a man
who does not make the world better